PRAISE FOR JONA~~1~~

"[Baumbach's] style lends itself well to settings of paranoid American noir, a miasma of sunglasses, pistols, and deadpan. For readers who enjoy that ilk, Baumbach delivers a nice, dark magic show."

—*Library Journal*

"Jonathan Baumbach has been a hero of mine since I started writing. I was then, and remain today, avid for novelists who push the limits of the novel's form without sacrificing its traditional human juices. Baumbach is just such a writer."

—Michael Cunningham, Pulitzer Prize–winning author of *The Hours*

THE LIFE AND TIMES OF MAJOR FICTION

"Jonathan Baumbach's retrospective collection showcases more than thirty years of work from an underappreciated writer. Baumbach employs a masterfully dispassionate, fiercely intelligent narrative voice whose seeming objectivity is always a faltering front for secret passion and despair.... In his recent stories, Baumbach relies less on the surreal effects he favored in the past, but he remains staunchly independent from the literary mainstream."

—*The New York Times Book Review*

"All fourteen stories in this collection are very good, and several are perfect gems. Baumbach, author of eight previous works of fiction, writes about ordinary people living essentially normal lives, but does so with such inventiveness and humor that their stories are transformed into something extraordinary. His characters bring fresh perspectives to bear on the world. They retell tales, veering from the truth, resculpting it to fit their mood or their audience.... Baumbach is not afraid to take risks with his fiction, and in this collection they pay off handsomely."

—*Publishers Weekly*

"Jonathan Baumbach is far more than the witty biographer of Major Fiction. The fact is, major fiction would be of lesser rank without him."

—Robert Coover, author of *The Brunist Day of Wrath*

"This wonderful book of stories, if only because of its title, invites comparison and then stands the test: this is major fiction. Which is not to say that the book is not hilarious—it is, and in a major way. Many of us who love contemporary fiction know that Jonathan Baumbach has been doing work of the first order for years; *The Life and Times of Major Fiction*, if there's any justice in the literary world, should bring him the wider recognition he deserves."

—Russell Banks, author of *Continental Drift* and *The Darling*

"*The Life and Times of Major Fiction* is a dazzling sampler of pleasures. Jonathan Baumbach writes gorgeous prose and he has a rare comic/tragic vision, especially of love."

—Hilma Wolitzer, author of *The Doctor's Daughter*

"This new collection of Baumbach's stories is fresh and startling, as ever. In *The Life and Times of Major Fiction*, he seems to reach new heights while cutting deep into the sense of loss that is both public and private. His engagement of the reader is so direct and so masterful that in response we cannot separate our hearts from our heads—and that is the enchantment of good fiction."

—Maureen Howard, author of *Facts of Life*

BABBLE

"Baumbach has a real gift for alchemizing fictional 'autobiography' into the pure gold of comic terror."

—*Newsweek*

"Humane, imaginative deftly composed..."

—*Boston Globe*

"Touching and wildly funny. Should be read by everyone."

—*Baltimore Sun*

"A brilliant conceit, endlessly inventive, a book of immense tenderness."

—Maureen Howard, author of *Facts of Life*

CHEZ CHARLOTTE AND EMILY

"A wonderful balance of ease and authority, subtlety and surprise, wisdom and playfulness...the balance is almost magical."

—Robert Coover, author of *The Brunist Day of Wrath*

"A brilliant novel...it is playful and unpredictable, a delightful instructive piece of reel life."

—*Hollins Critic*

DREAMS OF MOLLY

"It's comic, almost zany in tone, with a plot that is suspenseful even as it resists interpretation; reading it feels a bit like watching a David Lynch film."

—*New York Observer*

"A knock at the door of memory, and everything answers, all the more we didn't know we really did want to know. A beautiful book."

—Joseph McElroy, author of *Women and Men* and *Ancient History*

THE PAVILION
OF FORMER
WIVES

THE PAVILION OF FORMER WIVES

FICTIONS

JONATHAN BAUMBACH

DZANC BOOKS

5220 Dexter Ann Arbor Rd.
Ann Arbor, MI 48103
www.dzancbooks.org

Library of Congress Cataloging-in-Publication Data

Names: Baumbach, Jonathan, author.
Title: The pavilion of former wives / by Jonathan Baumbach.
Description: First editon. | Ann Arbor, MI : Dzanc Books, 2016.
Identifiers: LCCN 2016012143 | ISBN 9781941088616
Classification: LCC PS3552.A844 A6 2016 | DDC 813/.54--dc23
LC record available at https://lccn.loc.gov/2016012143

First US edition: December 2016
Interior design by Michelle Dotter

This is a work of fiction. Characters and names appearing in this work are a product of the author's imagination, and any similarity to real persons, living or dead, is coincidental and not intended by the author.

Printed in the United States of America

10   9   8   7   6   5   4   3   2   1

CONTENTS

To Aurora and Rohmer

THE PAVILION OF FORMER WIVES

One morning over coffee, a personals ad in B's favorite intellectual journal grabbed his attention. He wasn't actually reading the journal—he was thinking of what to do with the unsubscribed day ahead of him—when his eye, notoriously eager, arbitrarily browsed the ad. Its come-on line was, WHY FLY TO HORRORS THAT YOU KNOW NOT OF. Why indeed? The ad argued that a new relationship was likely to be as bad or worse than former disasters which might have been prevented through the wisdom of retrospect. It advocated visiting the digital Pavilion of Lost Loves at the New London County Fair, where, in a secure and protective environment, the seeker could revisit past relationships and, by rediscovering where they had hit the skids, possibly make right what had once gone terribly wrong.

"Crap!" said B, though later that day he got his car out of the high-rent garage where it spent the better part of its cloistered life and drove through oppressive traffic and seemingly endless road repair to New London. As it turned out, "Pavilion" was a misnomer. The whole enterprise—not easy to locate among the snarl of the fair—consisted of a small booth attended by a somewhat dowdy woman of uncertain age. Behind the booth, there was a closed door leading to an enclosure perhaps not much larger than a closet. After B presented himself, the woman, a Ms. Clover (her identity attested to by a nametag over her right breast), her thick hair in a tight bun, her glasses pink with transparent frames, said that she would be his guide on this trip into the domestic past. First, though, she had some questions for him. Names and dates mostly, basic information. His answers, some of them lies, were typed into the round-screened computer in front of her with a kind of energized slow motion.

"Is it only relationships with former wives that you wish to revisit?" she asked.

"I guess," he said. "I hadn't planned on anything else."

"We can do as many as five former lovers in a session," she said. "There's no extra charge."

He hadn't thought about the charge. "How much is this going to cost me?"

She studied him a moment before answering. "Ninety-five plus tax. You can use your debit card if you like."

"I hadn't planned on spending that much money," he said.

"That's too bad," she said, looking at him with what he took to be regret. "I'm offering you our off-season rate."

B considered returning to his car, which was on the far left side of the supplemental lot, and making the long trip through oppressive traffic and thwarting road repair to his lonely apartment with nothing to show for the time already invested in the enterprise before him.

Ms. Clover pretended not to look at him while waiting for his decision. "Did I mention," she said, "that the entrance fee is fully refundable less tax if you're not a hundred percent satisfied with your experience at the pavilion?"

"I think that's a good policy," he said, "though I don't remember you mentioning it before."

She gave her wrist a pantomime slap. "What were you thinking, Julia?" she said to herself. "Where was your head? If I didn't mention

it, and I will take your word for it on this occasion, you have the right
if you choose to take your trip down memory lane, as we sometimes
call it at the Pav, without the usual charge."

B felt the penalty for her mistake, even though he was the ben-
eficiary of it, was excessive. "I think I should pay something," he said.

After he unlocked the door with the key offered him, he warily
stepped into a room very much like the bedroom of the house he'd
lived in with his most recent former wife. The details, the colors of
the bedspread, the paintings on the wall, were remarkably close to the
overall picture memory offered. He briefly wondered how they were
able to get it this right on such short notice.

After a moment, an attractive woman who didn't quite resemble
his third wife (though dressed in her clothes) entered the room. "I
thought we agreed that you would stay downstairs," she said. "Isn't
that what we agreed on?"

It struck him that he had played out a scene very much like the
one he had just wandered into, though he had only the vaguest recollection of how he had responded to his wife's demand that he exile
himself. He had probably made some equally obnoxious remark in
return.

"What are we fighting about?" he asked in what he thought of as
a conciliatory tone.

"We're not fighting," she said. "We're just staying out of each other's way. If you insist on being up here, I'm going to stay downstairs."

The tone of her voice plus the substance of her remarks were
provoking, but B did what he could to keep his poise. He felt no
sympathy for her, though he stirred the ashes of former affection
hoping to find an ember.

"Well," she said, her arms folded in front of her, "are you going
or am I going?"

He had to shake himself to remember that this was not the real thing, merely a clever simulation. Still it was as painful in its own way, or so he suspected, as the first time around, which until this moment he had been pleased to forget. Anyway, since he was here in the spirit of melioration, he strove to be reasonable. "I'll go downstairs," he said, "but first tell me what I've done that seems so unforgivable to you."

She shook her head and stamped her foot. "Don't be such a woosie," she said. "No one respects a man who doesn't stand up for himself."

"Is that why you're angry at me, because I don't stand up for myself? I'm trying, don't you see, to make things better between us."

"But that's not what you're feeling, is it?"

It was true that B was angry at her—hadn't he been provoked?—though trying to keep his edginess from getting out of hand. "How the fuck do you know what I feel?" he asked.

She laughed. "I like you better this way. For a moment, I remembered what it was like to like you.... Look, don't get your hopes up."

"Is that what I was doing?"

"Just don't get your hopes up."

His anger at her slapped at the back of his head, pounded his chest, stomped on his toe. Was this the way it had been? B took a deep breath, petitioned for forgiveness, while she raised the level of her abuse. His cumulative anger, the unholy extent of it, frightened him. He imagined himself shaking her violently, pieces of her coming loose. Instead he picked up a rickety chair and smashed it against the wall. Though the flying chair had come nowhere near her, she visibly flinched. "Was I being a woosie then?" he asked, the question choosing him. He felt embarrassed and aggrieved by his tantrum.

"No," she said, "you were just being an asshole."

It seemed to him that exile almost anywhere, upstairs, downstairs, the next county, outer space—wasn't that why they got divorced?—was preferable to being in her company. Though he could no longer remember any of the details, he knew for a fact that they had once lived together amicably, had once in fact for an extended period of time been devoted to each other. And then what? It must have taken a while to reach this extreme point of disrepair in their marriage, bad feelings turning to worse and worse and worse. In any event, the paradigm of hell they were reenacting was clearly beyond salvage. B considered escaping through his original passage of entry, though a more complex instinct trapped him in the room.

What he did next was not premeditated, or if it was, he successfully short-circuited any awareness of intention. He sat down on the bed and put his head in his hands and let his eyes fill with tears as if they would have it no other way.

She studied him from wherever she was in the room, or so he sensed; he could just about feel the weight of her glance on his back. The next thing he knew she was seated next to him, an arm draped around his shoulders. "I'm sorry you feel so bad," she whispered, a secret perhaps from the self that hated him. B resented the superiority implied by her pity.

A sound of inchoate fury, a growling sound he had never heard himself make before, emerged from his throat, startling them both.

"What?" she asked.

He had no answer, had no idea what was at stake in her question. "I'm all right," he insisted despite compelling evidence otherwise. The comfort he took from her arm on his shoulder filled him with self-loathing. There was no longer any need to deny her charges against him: he was a woos, as she claimed. His head drooped against her shoulder in acknowledgment of woos-like defeat. Worse still, he had a hard-on with its own private agenda. His deepest wish, willfully unacknowledged, was to move into her womb and never leave. Enraptured by her embrace, he was blissfully immobile, though also desperate to get away. The word love sat on his tongue like a blister.

"It's not you I hate, it's myself," she said. "You see that, don't you?"

Lost in himself, he had no idea what she was getting at but her words nevertheless released him. Abruptly aware of his prick's agenda, he kissed her neck to foster its cause.

"I don't want that," she said, taking back her arm.

That was when he got up from the bed. "The hell with you," he said under his breath.

In the next moment, they were as far away from each other as the room allowed.

A few minutes later he was again standing in front of the Pavilion of Lost Loves facing Ms. Clover, who seemed to have found her way back to her former dowdy role. If he weren't still in despair over his revisited disaster, he might have been impressed at the lightning speed with which Clover had effected her costume change.

"What went wrong?" he asked her.

"I thought you knew," she said. "Look, I hope you won't take this the wrong way, but…"

"But what?"

"Well, not to make too much of it, you fucked up."

B was momentarily taken aback, but resisted offering any of the various barely credible defenses that immediately came to mind. "You know what," he said, "can we do this? I'd like to revisit this relationship fifteen years earlier. There were difficulties then—in fact, I was still married to someone else—but that was the high point of my relationship with Wife Three, as you call her in your notes."

"We can do that," she said, "but in the interest of full disclosure, I have to say if you visit Wife Three again it will count on your record as a visit to another lost love. If that's acceptable, I'm prepared to proceed. Are you sure that's what you want?"

"Yes," he said. "Yes." And though in the next moment he experienced a few twinges of regret, perpetually wary of getting what he wanted, he held his ground. "I think so," he added.

"After I go through the door, I'd like you to count slowly to three hundred before making your entrance. Okay?"

"I have a watch," he said, checking his wrist to verify his claim. "You're asking me to wait five minutes, isn't that it?"

"For best results," she said, "please follow instructions to the letter. We feel that counting adds a necessary human element." And then as she closed the door behind her, he heard her whisper, "One... two...three..."

B counted to sixty, which was tedious enough, then let four more minutes tick off on his watch, then he counted to twenty-five before opening the door. He found himself at the bottom of a long stairwell and, not wanting to think about how Clover managed the trick, climbed up the four flights to the apartment his third wife lived in for a period before she was his third wife, and knocked at the door. He heard some remote signs of life in the apartment so that he knew that the lack of response was not an indicator of no one being home. He knocked again. "What is it?" a woman's voice inquired.

"It's me," he said, which produced a laugh.

"Just a minute," she said. He heard the door unlatch from the inside, followed by the scuffling of steps fading into the distance.

"It's open," a faint voice called to him.

When he stepped inside into her loft space—an extended room with a kitchen tucked into the far wall—his not-yet-third wife was in bed reading a magazine, or at least offering that impression. "I didn't expect you," she said. "I haven't seen you in a while and I thought, you know, maybe he doesn't want to see me."

"I called to say I was coming," he said.

"That's true, you did," she said. "I think there was something in the way you said it that made me think you wouldn't come. Some reluctance, as if someone were holding on to you when you were talking to me." She sighed with notable conviction. "Sweetheart, how long can you stay?" She held out a ghostly hand in his direction, which he only noticed as it was being withdrawn. B had been looking at his watch.

"I have to go in about two hours," he said. He sat down on the edge of the bed like a tourist.

"I've missed you," she said. "Lie next to me. I want to feel you. How else do I know you're real?"

The idea of making love to a stranger (Ms. Clover) performing the role of his former wife made him uncomfortable, though he had what he thought of as a commemorative hard-on. Moreover, the resemblance was compelling. He took off his shoes and got under the covers with her.

"Please hold me," she said.

In the next moment, they were pressed against each other. She held onto him as if he were the only thing that kept her from drowning and eventually, his choices narrowing down, they fucked with a conflicting mix of caution and urgency.

They exchanged fluids, songs, and vows of love not quite in that order.

It was over and he still had an hour and a half left to his visit and so he asked her what she'd been up to.

"I spend much of my time thinking about you making love to your wife," she said. "I tend to focus on things that make me unhappy. Other than that.... You deny that there's anything between you and I believe you, or try to believe you. I won't say any more because I don't want to be a nag, but it's hard for me living like this. It feels unreal to me."

"I can see that," he said. He wondered if it was possible to love someone and at the same time want desperately to get away from them.

"I live for the times we get together," she said.

"It's the same for me," he said, and while they were hugging he noticed that he had fifty-five minutes left on the duration of his visit.

"Would you like to go for a walk?" he asked.

"Is that what you want to do? You were going to read me the first chapter of your novel."

"It isn't quite finished," he said.

"So you didn't bring it with you."

"No."

"I'm willing to look at it in an unfinished form."

"I'll bring it next time I come."

"I don't think we should see each other again until you're free. I've been wanting to say that to you but it just seemed too hard not to see you. What do you think? When we come to each other, let's do it without any baggage."

"It makes a kind of sense," he said. He was still lying next to her and his prick indicated it was ready for another go. "It will be hard."

This was not the particular day of this otherwise memorable period in his life he had hoped to re-explore.

"I don't know if I can keep to it," she said. "Do you think you can?"

When he bent over to kiss her, she turned her head away. "One last time," he said, kissing her ear to plead his case.

"You're going to have to be stronger than that," she said. "We're both going to have to be stronger to keep to our agreement."

He got out of bed and searched the floor for his clothes.

"You don't have to leave right away," she said. "This may turn out to be our last time together. You still have some time left, don't you?"

She patted a spot on the bed, an invitation to return. He avoided looking at his watch, though he sensed his time was short in every sense. It was her habit to be seductive moments before he had to leave in the hope of prolonging his visit.

He was going to say that it would have to be quick, but he censored himself to avoid provoking her displeasure. When he sat down on the bed she removed his blue-striped boxers, which he had only moments before reacquired. She went down on him, though barely long enough for his vacillating prick to reassert itself. Then she parted her legs like the red sea and he entered her like a grieving survivor with aggressive good faith and divided heart, an unacknowledged part of his consciousness wondering how he would explain himself on his belated return home. Eventually, aware of time's unseemly haste, B rolled over to allow her the top position. She sang her song before he did and he made an effort to focus on his receding pleasure. "Are you all right, my love?" she asked, which was the question that brought him off.

After a few moments of controlled impatience, he whispered that he really had to leave, as much as he would prefer staying with her. Had to leave.

"Then stay," she said, still on top of him, her arms around his neck.

He was tired, he was beyond tired, but he released himself, kissed her on the top of her head, and slid out from under her.

"It won't kill you to stay a few minutes longer," she said.

"I can come by Friday morning, if that's all right," he said.

"That's not all right," she said, holding onto him from the back as he tried to dress himself.

"Then it'll have to wait until Monday," he said.

"No," she said.

"No?"

"We've agreed not to see each other until you're free," she said. "Isn't that what we agreed?"

When he got out the door, forty-seven minutes later than the time he had set himself earlier in the evening, he was almost pleased at the prospect of not seeing her again, until he remembered he had married her a year and a half after her resolve to stop seeing him and that they had actually lived together for twelve years.

In the next moment, he was standing in front of the Pavilion booth, facing the prodigious Clover, who was prepared to take him on the third of his five allotted visits.

"That's okay," he said to her. "I want to waive my rights to the other visits. I've had enough, though this is no reflection on your service. You people—" He wondered where the others were. "—were as good as your ad promised." He shook her hand, not knowing how else to say goodbye.

"Well, thank you for coming," she said, handing him her card, which she said would serve as a rain check for his three unused visits to lost loves if he ever planned to return.

When he got home—the traffic if anything slightly worse than it was on the trip out—his loneliness (his loneness) seemed an under-valued condition.

He didn't know whether to call it a date or not, but if it wasn't a date, how else might it be described? Three weeks or so after his visit to the Pavilion, looking for something else among the debris on the top of his dresser, he stumbled on the card Ms. Clover had given him on his abrupt departure. There was a handwritten New York City phone number underneath the official Pavilion number, which he hadn't noted before. It seemed like the kind of request any reasonable man would honor.

They met at an obscure vegetarian restaurant in an unfashionable neighborhood a few blocks north of Soho.

If some sadistic torturer were pulling out his fingernails one by one to elicit an answer, he still wouldn't be able to say why he had phoned her or why, in the course of their conversation, he had suggested they meet for dinner. He might have confessed without conviction that his reasons lay somewhere in the nether territory between curiosity and loneliness.

He was early—it was his nature to be early—and he was stationed at a corner table with a view of the entrance, trying to remember what the person he was expecting might look like when she came through the door. Despite the vantage of his seat and his sense of being alert to whomever entered the restaurant, when a stylish younger woman not wearing glasses and claiming to be Julia Clover approached his table, he had not seen her coming. The brisk, familiar handshake before seating herself across from him was as close as she got to confirming her credentials.

"I'm glad you came," he said, trying to locate the face he knew within the face he didn't without seeming to stare. "I don't think I made a very good impression at the Pavilion. In fact, I'm sure I didn't."

She shrugged and turned her attention to her menu. "If I thought you were hopeless, I wouldn't have come," she said.

"Do you date many of your clients?" he asked, not so much interested in the answer as having something to say.

"Virtually none," she said.

It was later, after they had ordered their meals and seemed to have gotten more comfortable with each other, that B asked the hitherto avoided question that he assumed was already in the air between them. "I suppose you wouldn't want to tell me how you're able on short notice to create such convincing scenes from your clients' pasts. It's very impressive."

"Thank you, I guess," she said.

"Have you trained as an actress?"

"I never took any courses," she said, "if that's what you mean."

He meant no more than he asked and perhaps even less. "You don't give away much," he said. "You know a lot more about me than I know about you."

"What do you want to know?"

"Well, who is Julia Clover?"

She offered him a sly smile and held her arms out, framing the picture. "What you see is what there is. Do you want to know where I went to school? Is that what you want? Julia Clover, *c'est moi*."

B didn't know what he wanted, but whatever it was he was not close to having it satisfied. "How old are you?" he asked.

"Older than I look," she said. "And that's not a very polite question."

Feeling thwarted, he thought to mention that the Ms. Clover at the Pavilion offered a very different impression than the Julia Clover in the fashionable black sweater sitting across from him, phrased and rephrased the observation so as not to give offense, but ended up swallowing whatever it was he had been chewing on.

Moments after she had ordered dessert, she excused herself to go to the bathroom. He watched with grudging admiration as she moved among the tables toward the back of the restaurant, feeling an ache of loss at her impending absence.

He knew instinctively that she would not return and regretted how badly he had handled their brief time together.

So when she did return, it was as if he was being offered a second chance. A second chance for what, he wondered.

He made conversation, told her things about himself she may not have known as she worked at her cranberry tart, circling the edges as she inched her way inside.

After she had all she wanted, at least a third of it left for the kitchen, he paid the bill with an American Express card.

They shook hands outside the restaurant as prelude to each going his or her own way, which in this case were divergent directions.
He walked half a block, then turned around and called after her,
"I intend to use my rain checks," he shouted to her. "You'll be seeing
me again."

She seemed not to have heard him, took another few steps before
turning to face him. In the next moment, she was running in his
direction, her heels clacking like castanets against the pavement. For
an untested moment, he thought of glancing behind him. Instead,
he took a brief step in her direction and, filled with intimations of
regret, a history of sinking ships flashing before his eyes, offered her
his hand.

ACTING OUT

Now that Jay had agreed to the joint session with her therapist, Lois couldn't remember why she had favored the idea in the first place. It was one of those things you did, which is what she told Lorrie over the phone, so that afterward you could say you had done everything (or something) to save your dying marriage. She wondered if she had ever loved Jay—that is, she could no longer remember having loved him, but there was something between them, some intricate bond, that seemed resistant to violations no matter how unforgivable. All she wanted, after all, was to get free of him, and then afterward they could salvage or not whatever dregs of their relationship remained.

Jay, on the other hand, said he was willing to change if necessary to save their marriage.

"No one changes after forty-five," she said.

"Who said?" he said.

"I can't remember anyone who has," she said, dipping her toe briefly into the well of memory. "Can you?"

"Maybe what we're talking about is not the incapacity to change," he said, "but a failure of memory."

She hated it, totally despised it, when he pretended to be smart. At the same time or perhaps a moment afterward she had a quiver of recollection—a subliminal flash—of having felt something other than indifference for him.

For their first session, they sat in parallel chairs about twenty feet apart facing the therapist, who was in an impressive high-backed armchair in a slightly elevated part of the room.

"Is there some agreement as to who goes first?" Leo asked, looking at neither of them in such a way as to give each the impression of being the one he was urging.

Jay was the first to speak. "I don't mind if she starts," he said.

"I'd prefer going second," she said. "He's the one who believes in talk."

"In that case," Leo said, "that's the way we'll do it. So Jay, what's your view of why your marriage isn't working?"

"Why does she get to go second?" Jay said. "Is it because she's a woman?"

"I thought you were both in agreement as to the order here," Leo said. "When you offered her the opportunity to go first, I assumed you took it to be the favored position. If it wasn't, why did you make it sound as if you were doing her a favor?"

"Because that's the way he is," she said.

Leo gestured for her to stop whatever else she was planning to add. "Let's hear what Jay has to say, shall we?"

Jay stood up, collected his coat, but then seemed to change his mind from whatever to whatever. "You're both right," he said. "I'm a terrible person and I'm choked with regret."

"That's a bit easy," Leo said. "Don't you think?"

"I'm sorry about that too," he said. "I tend to let myself off too easily and I'm sorry. Okay?"

"He isn't really sorry," Lois said.

"You're probably right about that," he said, "but look, I'm really sorry that I'm not really sorry. What about you, LL? Is there anything you're sorry about?"

"That's not a real question," she said, "and you know it. Do you want me to say that I'm sorry I married you? All right, I'll say that I'm sorry I married you."

Leo looked around as if there were another person in the room with them, possibly dangerous, that he hadn't seen before. "Let's stop here," he said, "and we'll continue next Wednesday at the same time."

Jay, who had been standing, his coat folded over his arm, sat down. "We haven't even decided who goes first," he said.

While Jay wrote the therapist a check for the truncated session, Lois mumbled, "Thank you, Leo," and made her way out the door.

There was an antique shop a few doors down and she occupied herself studying the unusual face of an oversized wall clock in the window, figuring Jay would be out in a few minutes and they would travel back on the subway together. She didn't see him come out, though sensed his approaching presence, feeling a sugar rush of affection for him, arming herself with a slightly ironic remark.

For his part, Jay noticed his disaffected wife waiting for him and decided to cross the street to avoid her, pretending to the unseen observer that he was in a huge hurry to get somewhere.

When, on turning her head, she noticed him rushing from her, she wanted to call out that she was not as frightful as he imagined.

SECOND SESSION

"If anything's going to get accomplished, we're going to need to give these meetings some structure," Leo said. "Lois, I'm going to ask you to speak for no more than five minutes. At which point, Jay can either respond to what you've said or use the allotted five minutes to present his own grievances. On the second go-around, I'd like you

each to address what the other has said. Are there any questions before we begin?… If not, let's get to it. Lois."

"It's easier if I get up," she said, though she remained seated. "I
don't think I'll need five minutes to say what I have to say. Actually,
I don't know why I'm here. For a while now, I kind of thought that,
despite our persistent problems, it was worth making whatever effort
was necessary to continue to get along. I no longer feel that way.
That's all. Well, one other thing: whatever feelings I once had for Jay
are gone. It's like one morning, they put on their coats and scarves
and went out the door. I feel my own growth as a person has been
inhibited by this marriage. That's all. I don't want it anymore. I don't
want to be in this marriage. That's all I have."

Leo seemed to be waiting for Lois to continue, but after a few
minutes he pointed his finger at Jay, who seemed to be looking the
other way. "Jay?"

Jay stood up. He had something written on a card that he held
up in front of him. "I was going to say that I would do whatever I
could to keep us together, but that seems foolish now, doesn't it?" He
sat down, resisted putting his head in his hands.

Leo looked over at Lois, who made a point of avoiding eye
contact, and waited for someone, perhaps even himself, to break
the silence. "It might be useful," he said to her, "if you were more
specific about what you want and feel you're not getting from your
marriage."

"What I want, okay, is that Jay accept the fact that the marriage
is over," she said.

"Why should Jay's acceptance or not make a difference?" Leo
asked her.

"It just does," she said.

"She wants to hurt me," Jay said, "but in a way that protects her
from feeling bad about herself. She hates the sight…"

Leo was quick to intervene. "Let her speak for herself, please," he said. "The two of you seem to know more about the other's feelings than your own. I understand that your feelings about Jay are intuitive, Lois, but it would be useful here if you gave some examples of what seems to be the problem."

"He doesn't want to hear them," she said.

'Then tell them to me," Leo said. "I want to hear them."

She had a hundred grievances against Jay, she had a litany of grievances—they often came to mind unbidden like the hypnogenic lyric of some ancient detergent commercial—but at the moment she couldn't come up with one that didn't seem hopelessly trivial. "He's only interested in me as an extension of himself," she said.

"That's not specific enough," Leo said.

"He doesn't clean up after himself," she said. "He leaves crumbs all over the apartment, which I end up having to deal with."

"What do you say to that?" Leo asked, turning his attention to Jay.

"I'm not sure what you're referring to," Jay said.

The role she was performing laughed. "You see what I mean," she said.

Leo reiterated in paraphrase Lois's complaint about his messiness.

"She's probably right about that in general," Jay said, "but I've been better about it recently. I think even Lois would acknowledge that I've been trying."

"Too little, too late," she said.

"Let's put this into perspective," Leo said. "If, say, overnight, Jay no longer left messes that he didn't clear up, became a sudden exemplar of neatness and consideration, would that alter your feelings toward him?"

Lois wanted to say that it might, but since she didn't believe it, felt the dishonesty of any such assertion, she said nothing, or rather mumbled something that was susceptible to a near infinite variety of interpretations.

"What Leo's saying," Jay said, "is that the example you gave represents a petty annoyance and is hardly a significant factor in your disaffection toward me."

"I don't think that's what he's saying," she said. "Is that what you're saying, Leo?"

"Is there anything Jay can do or not do that would make you reconsider your decision to separate?" Leo asked.

"What about her?" Jay interrupted, suddenly outraged. "Why is this whole discussion about my changing?"

"There's nothing he can do," she said, "nothing that would make the slightest bit of difference."

"I hear you," Leo said. "Jay, what changes would you like to see Lois make?"

Jay started, then stopped himself. "Well, for openers," he said, "she can stop fucking Roger or whoever it is she's been seeing on the sly."

Leo seemed unfazed by the revelation. "And if she stopped," he said, "would that make a difference?"

"I'm sorry I said that," Jay said.

"What are you sorry about?" Leo asked. "It was something you felt, wasn't it? You meant it, didn't you?"

Jay looked over at Lois, who seemed to have shut down. "I didn't want to embarrass you," he said.

"I thought you thought I was shameless," she said, and seemed, until she took a deep breath, on the verge of giving in to feelings she was hours away from acknowledging.

———

THIRD SESSION

They arrived at the therapist's office together and Jay suggested that she go in by herself and that he would loiter in the lobby of the building, kill a few minutes, before making his appearance.

"You're joking, right?"

"Well, I don't see any reason to throw Leo off his game."

"As Leo would tell you, and as I'm sure you know, that's exactly what you do want. Denial is a form of admission. What's Leo's game, in your opinion?"

"I'm here to find out," he said.

She laughed. "Shouldn't we tell him things are better?"

"What do you think?"

They entered Leo's office at the same time, though not quite together, made their appearance in single file, Lois the first to enter.

As they sat down in their respective seats, Leo looked over his glasses from one to the other, then jotted something down in the small notebook he always seemed to have on the table in front of him. "People, I'd like to try something a little different today," he said. "I'd like to have you switch roles—Lois, you take on the role of Jay, and Jay, you present yourself as Lois—for the next twenty minutes."

Lois looked skeptical, while Jay seemed vaguely amused.

"So Jay, putting yourself in Lois's shoes, I'd like you to present your grievances toward your husband…"

"She wears a 7B," Jay said. "There's no way I could get my feet in her shoes without cutting off my toes."

Leo ignored him. "And Lois," he said, "I'd like you to begin to imagine yourself as Jay. I'll give you both a few minutes to focus and then Lois—that is, Jay as Lois—will start. Otherwise, it will be the same format as last week. Once we start, I'd like you both to stay in character. Any questions?"

"I don't know, Leo," Lois said. "I'm not comfortable with this."

"Let's give it a try, okay, and see how it goes," Leo said.

"I'd prefer standing," Jay said slyly, getting up and then sitting down. "One of the things about Jay that makes my hair curl is that he is incapable of empathy. That's all I have to say at the moment."

"Jay," Leo said, pointing to Lois.

"Lois tends to be a perfectionist," she said, "and so tends to be what I call hypercritical. The way I see it, there's nothing I can do to please her no matter how many times I apologize for being oblivious. She has an idea of how people should be and if you don't live up to that idea, you're in trouble. You never know exactly where you stand with her."

"Could you give us an example of what you mean?"

"An example? Well, one night after a hard closing, she comes home from work and finds me sprawled out on the couch, watching TV—a basketball game, most likely—and she says something like, 'You're supposed to be working on your book, not watching TV, aren't you?' And then it comes out that I'd neglected to do the little bit of shopping she had asked me to do and I get some more grief from her. I don't answer and then I offer an unfelt apology, but when she keeps at it I put my coat on and go out for a walk. Some hours later, when I come back, I find her talking on the phone to someone I think I have reason to assume is her lover."

"How does that make you feel?" Leo asks.

"How does that make me feel? I let her know how angry I am by knocking over a few chairs and then I order her to get off the phone. It's not the best way to handle it, but I have to do something and I haven't the faintest idea what else to do. I'm bigger than she is and I don't see why I shouldn't get my way."

Jay waited a few minutes before speaking. "Look, I'm not going to let myself be bullied by him in my own house. I have a right to talk to whoever I please. His behaving like a jerk only makes me more determined. His bad behavior, which I may have pro-voked—you get to know the right buttons—is embarrassing to me. He knows I hate scenes. And so I get off the phone, which makes me hate him even more, but not before telling my friend that I'll call him back."

"Do you ever, after the dust has cleared, talk about what went on?" Leo asked Lois.

"Not usually. Mostly we avoid each other. One of us goes in the bedroom and the other stays in the living room."

"What happens the next morning?" Leo asked Jay.

"I don't as a rule talk much in the morning, and when we do talk we tend to be excruciatingly polite, as if one wrong word might cause irreparable damage."

"Do you have breakfast together?" Leo asked Lois.

"I…excuse me…Lois doesn't eat breakfast. She has coffee and sometimes a toasted bialy but it's not a sit-down breakfast. On the other hand, I have designer cold cereal in the morning and tend to read the sports page while making music chewing my granola."

"If you don't discuss your fights, how do you ever reconcile your differences?" Leo asked Jay.

"Time heals," Jay said, "and sometimes doesn't."

Lois cut in just as Jay was completing his sentence. "My policy is to ignore problems and hope they go away," she said.

"When I feel wronged, I can be absolutely unforgiving," Jay said, "and it's possible that Jay has been burned too much to be willing to risk making a gesture he knows will be scorned."

Lois pursed her lips. "I guess when the going's tough, I don't have much backbone, do I?"

Jay picked up a flyer that had been lying on the table and folded it into a paper airplane.

Leo's bearded face showed a minor crack of concern and he suggested, after Jay had launched the paper airplane in Lois's direction and Lois had stared daggers at Jay in return, that it might be a good idea to stop the role playing at this point and return to their former selves. "I'll give you a few minutes to get back into your own heads."

"This was useful," Lois said. "When he was going on about me being hypercritical and unforgiving, I got the impression he was really talking about himself. I learned something from that."

"Hey, weren't we both talking about ourselves?" Jay said.

"You're so clever," she said. "Why hadn't I ever noticed that before?"

"You're the princess of snide," he said. "Look, I'm sorry I threw the plane in your direction. It wasn't really meant to hit you, it was to make you aware there was someone else in the room."

"You never say anything that means anything," she said. "Why is that? You are the prince of self-justifying incoherence."

Jay got out of his chair with apparent difficulty, as if fighting some kind of invisible resistance, and retrieved his coat.

"Why don't you just leave," Lois said.

Leo turned his head just enough to glance at the clock on the wall.

"We still have some time left, people," he said.

FOURTH SESSION

There is no fourth session.

SEATTLE

For weeks they argued, as if the terrifying unimaginable were at stake, over something that had happened (or had not happened) fifteen years back. Or perhaps seventeen years back, as Genevieve continued to insist. The dispute concerned a trip they had taken to Seattle—that much was sometimes agreed on—in which they had both behaved badly, a trip that had very nearly ended in the dissolution of a long-term marriage. It had come back to Josh in barely discernible disguise, provoked into memory by a startlingly vivid dream.

When he woke in a tattered rage, he replayed the dream in his head, not wanting to lose it as he had lost so much else in recent years, juggling its shapeless fragments in the imaginary air while waiting for Genevieve to open her eyes.

Finally, outmaneuvered by his own impatience, he woke her.

"I just had this disturbing dream…" he started.

She anticipated what came next. "And you want me to listen to it? Is that what this is about?"

"You were in the dream," he said.

"Was I?"

He couldn't remember when it started or even precisely how it started or if it had always been this way. He would have something in his hand or there was something in his sight he was thinking of picking up, something—whatever—he had plans for, and then in the next moment it was nowhere. Once it had vanished, he could look everywhere for it, he could tear the house apart, and not find it. How furious it made him, furious both at himself and the disappeared object, his reading glasses, say, or a book he thought he might want to read, furious at being thwarted. Genevieve hated his rages, but what else could he do, it was the only revenge powerlessness allowed.

Shortly after that, or perhaps concurrently, was Josh's burgeoning failure to come up with words (sometimes names) that had previously been available to him. It was his habit to do the *Times* crossword puzzle every night before going to sleep. His skill, which he secretly prided himself on, began to fail him, answers that were on the edge of memory denying him access. And more than once, perhaps even several times, he lost the names of people he knew perfectly well when running into them unexpectedly. If he worked at it, which he did—it was almost all he did—he was certain he could defeat the problem.

"I'll listen to your dream after I have my coffee," she said.

He followed her into the kitchen impatiently, rehearsing the opening of the dream in his head. They were riding in a rented car, an Audi wagon, going to a party at an old, sometime friend's house.

"I have a feeling I know how this is going to end up," she said, sipping her coffee.

"I was anxious in the dream," he said, "because the host was someone you had a one-night stand with in Seattle. I wanted to turn back, though the trip had its own momentum."

"I never had a one-night stand with anyone in Seattle, for God's sake," she said. "Who did you have in mind?"

"The trip seemed to go on forever, though it was supposed to be three hours at most. Maybe we should go back, I said. It'll be longer going back, you said. Let's just get there and get it over with. Then suddenly the house appeared—it was as if it were in the middle of the road—and we had to pull over to the side not to run into it. Pulling over, we slid into a ditch and you said you knew this would happen. I promised you I would find a way out, but you seemed skeptical. Anyway, we got out of the car and went into the house without knocking or ringing the bell. We were obviously very late because the party seemed in its last stages, couples lying on the floor, drunk or asleep, a few having sex in what seemed like slow motion. The hostess appeared—the man's wife—and she said to make ourselves at home, but that she was sorry to say all the good wine had already been consumed. I had brought a bottle but it was still in the car and I excused myself to go out and retrieve it. Don't leave me, you whispered, but I went out anyway, stopping at the door for a moment to embrace the hostess, whose name I had forgotten.

"And then I was in the car, looking under the seat for the bottle of good wine I had brought. I came up with a dusty bottle of Pinot Blanc I had never seen before—it was not the bottle I remembered taking—and handed it to the hostess, who was on the floor of the car on her knees next to me. 'I know this wine,' she said to me. 'It was my absolute favorite before I quit drinking and carousing altogether. I don't know how to thank you. Will a long, lingering kiss do the trick?'

"I didn't think an answer was appropriate. Then we got out of the car and started back to the house. She took me around the side, where there was a picture window, and we looked into the master bedroom together, her small breasts pressing against my back. There was a couple on the bed, fooling around, his head under her skirt and she said, 'That's my husband and your wife.' It was odd because I didn't recognize you at first. 'What do you want to do about it?' she asked me."

————

"Is that it?" Genevieve asked.

"There was more, but the rest comes and goes. The point is, it was just like that time at the party in Seattle where the hostess and I found you in the upstairs guest room with her husband. He had been a high school sweetheart or something of the sort."

"I have no idea what you're talking about," she said. "That never happened. When is this supposed to have happened?"

"The trip, don't you remember that terrible trip we took—we had picked up your mother's car in Annapolis—I don't remember what it was doing there—and we were delivering it to them in Seattle. It was fifteen years ago. I never wanted to go. We fought over everything. Don't you remember?"

"I don't remember because it never happened. Josh, we haven't been to Seattle together in seventeen years."

"It could have been seventeen years ago, but it doesn't seem as if that much time has passed. You asked my forgiveness, don't you remember, and you said it would never happen again."

Genevieve laughed. "You're out of your mind.... I didn't mean that the way it came out. If anything, you're conflating several different events. Yes?"

"No," he said. "I'm right about this."

She left the kitchen and, after deciding not to, he followed her up the stairs. When he reached her—she was in her study, sitting at her computer—he couldn't remember what he wanted to say.

"I can't live with your suspicions," she told him the next day or the day after that.

"This was fifteen years ago," he said.

"You're the most ungenerous man I've ever known," she said. "It didn't even happen."

He waited until she was sitting at the table to make the point he had been thinking about much of the previous night. He had lost it temporarily but now it was at memory's fingertips. "If it never happened, why does it disturb you if I mention it?"

She had no answer and then she did. "How would you like it," she said, "if I constantly reminded you of the time twelve years ago that you hit me."

"I never," he said, aggrieved. "I don't remember ever hitting you."

"That doesn't mean it never happened," she said, "does it? You have an awful temper and you know it."

He remembered the car, an oversized Chevrolet that had a habit of stalling at red lights. And so he brought it up to her when they talked again several hours later, reminded her of the car's various unnerving tics.

"My mother never drove a Chevrolet," she said.

"If it wasn't a Chevrolet," he said, "what was the car we drove across the country? It was a blue and white Chevrolet."

"That was a different time," she said. "Anyway, I never went to high school in Seattle."

It was possible that the boy he had caught her with in Seattle resembled her high school sweetheart. The phone interrupted this thought and he took the occasion to answer it. It was someone from their bank, offering to sell him some pointless new service no one in his right mind could possibly want. It was presented to him as a favor they owed him for being such a good customer. Even after he said no thank you, the voice at the other end continued her rehearsed spiel. "Damn it," he said. "When I say no, I mean no."

"When you say no, you often change your mind afterward," she said. This was Genevieve, not the woman on the phone, whom he had temporarily shut out of his life five minutes earlier.

When he took Magoo, their Airedale, out for his evening walk, he tried to conjure up Genevieve's mother's errant Chevrolet. No details answered his quest. Maybe it wasn't a Chevrolet, though unless he had lost his mind altogether there had been a car they had picked up in Annapolis and driven to Seattle.

The next time Josh approached her to make some debater's point, she could no longer remember the particulars of their long-running argument. He caught her at the refrigerator door, struggling against residual vagueness, wondering what urgency had brought her there. "Are you ready to admit that I was right?" she said.

"I didn't want to make the trip to Seattle," he said, "because I never enjoyed myself in your mother's house."

She peered into the refrigerator, hoping that something in the picture would remind her that she had come on its errand.

"My mother always spoke highly of you," she said. "That was until she stopped remembering who you were. She actually encouraged me to marry you, though of course I never did what she wanted and she knew that like the back of her hand."

"It was your mother," he said, "who invited that guy—your high school sweetheart—to lunch with us. He was in Seattle on some business trip or he had just moved there and he phoned your mother to find out where you were."

She took a container of milk from the refrigerator, which seemed as good a choice as any. It might have been that she was planning to make a pot of coffee. "You're saying he, whoever, called my mother."

"Yes," he said, "and she invited him over."

"She invited him to the house in Seattle? That's an odd thing for her to do. Where was I?"

"You were there," he said angrily. "You were already there."

"Was I? And where were you?"

"On the outside, looking in."

It had been dark for almost two hours and they were still driving around looking for an acceptable place to stop for the night. Genevieve was in one of her moods. None of the motels they passed in the seemingly endless sprawl of this one-street small town impeding their progress appealed to her. "You make the choice, Josh," she said.

"What about this one?" he said. They were approaching a row of nondescript cabins. According to the flickering sign, the place was called Dew Drop Inn.

"Oh, Josh," she said, "that's so depressing. We've passed by places that were nicer than this." He pulled into the parking space next to the office. "I'm not staying here," she muttered.

He went into the brightly lit office without her and rented 6A with his American Express card, though the proprietor warned that a drunk trucker tended to come by around 3 a.m. and was likely to knock on the door, insisting the place was his. "All you have to do," the woman said, "is to keep your door locked and pay no attention to him. After a while, he gets discouraged. You'll be making a big mistake if you answer the door."

When he returned to the car, already regretting his decision to pay for the room, Genevieve was a notable absence. He lounged in the driver's seat for a few minutes, dozing, waiting with willed indifference for her return, assuming nothing, assuming she had gone off looking for a bathroom or had decided to leave him forever. When he could no longer sit still, he evacuated the car to look for her. Having no idea where to look, he headed toward the diner they had passed a block or so back, his best guess, hurrying, speed-walking, breathing hard, running.

He was so intent on getting there he nearly ran over her in the dark, as she came slowly toward him. "Is that you, Josh?" she said. "I got us some coffee."

"Damn you," he said.

She woke up the next morning with something on her mind that concerned Joshua. She woke up remembering how fond she was of him, which was, she suspected, an abrupt change in the weather. For months, perhaps years, she had been nursing the hope that he would silently disappear. As soon as she got into her forest-green terrycloth bathrobe, which he had given her last Christmas (there were some things she didn't forget), she intended to go downstairs—she heard someone banging around in the kitchen—and tell whomever it was (who else could it be?) about her discovery. A detour to the bathroom to pee and to brush her teeth interceded. By the time Genevieve reached the kitchen, she could still remember she had something she wanted to tell Joshua, but not what it was.

"I made coffee," he said when she approached, "but I finished most of it."

"There's something I have to tell you," she said.

He took a coffee mug from the cupboard for her, filling it almost halfway with what remained of the pot he had brewed. He was embarrassed to tell her that there was no longer any milk.

She improvised her news. "I need to know," she said, "why you leave fingerprints on the bathroom towels."

"So we'll have a subject for conversation," he said, "other than Seattle, which you won't discuss."

"Do you expect the fingerprints to go on forever?" she asked.

"Not forever," he said. "If he wasn't your high school sweetheart, who was the man in the bedroom with you in Seattle?"

She left the room abruptly, having no interest in the turn the conversation had taken, but then returned momentarily with an appropriate response. "Whoever he was, he didn't leave fingerprints on clean towels," she said.

"If he was such a paragon, why didn't you run off with him when you had the chance?"

She was on to him now. "You brought him around, didn't you, so you would have an excuse to get rid of me. That's so like you."

"It was your mother, not me, who brought him into the house."

"So you say," she said, "but it could have been you who told Mother to invite him over. This happened where?"

"It was in Seattle."

"No way."

"I know it was Seattle. That was where your mother was living at the time."

"I'll tell you why you're wrong," she said. "My mother never would have allowed it, never in a million years. You know what I think? I think the person in the bedroom with me was you."

He left an unfinished sentence on his computer screen to ask Genevieve if she would like to go for a walk.

"Do I like taking walks?" she asked.

He couldn't remember the last time they had walked together, but he wouldn't have asked if there was no chance that she would accept. Rejection had never been high on his list of priorities. "It's your call," he said.

"My call?" she said. "Really my call? I'll tell you what. I'll walk with you if you promise not to tell me your dream. Let's not walk too far, all right?" She took his arm, then gave it back and disappeared to find her coat. Her searches always took longer than anticipated. She remembered that she hated to feel cold while whoever she was with seemed not to mind.

When she returned, she asked him if he knew why she had her coat on.

"We were going to go for a walk if I made a certain promise," he said.

"Did you really think I didn't know we were going for a walk?" she said. "I knew we were going for a walk. What was this promise you were going to make?"

"I'm not making any promises," he said.

"You make too many promises as it is," she said, which offended him momentarily and then amused him to no end. It seemed to him the wittiest thing she had said to him in ages.

His extended amusement, which bent him over, disconcerted her. She wondered if she had meant what she said, whatever it was, as a joke all along. She laughed in echo, not wanting to seem out of it.

He was still smiling at her remark as they started their walk hand in hand in the general direction of their local park.

"How much farther do we have to go?" she asked.

"We haven't gone anywhere, sweetheart," he said. "Do you want to go back? We'll go back if you want to go back."

"I don't want to do anything that makes you angry," she said, "though everything I do makes you angry."

"Let's go back," he said, taking back his hand.

"I don't want to go back," she said. "Do you even know the way back? You're always getting us lost. You know that's true."

"Of course I know the way," he said, looking over his shoulder to see if their house was still in the distance behind them. "And when did I ever get you lost?"

A much younger couple with a baby in a stroller excused themselves to edge their way by. "Do you know where the park is?" Genevieve asked the woman.

"It's where we're going," the woman said. "You can follow us." Genevieve admired the baby and thanked the couple.

"I know where the park is," Josh said when they were alone. "You didn't have to ask anyone."

After a while they came to the corner of their extended block and Josh saw or thought he saw the park in the distance, the couple with the stroller framed in the entrance, which confirmed him in his view of himself as someone in charge of his own life. He had a reputation even in better days for having an unreliable sense of direction. It was strictly the judgment of others. Insofar as he could remember, he had always gotten where he was going.

"Do you have any idea where we're going?" Genevieve asked.

"We're just taking a walk," he said.

"I suppose that's all right," she said.

Eventually, the park moved toward them in its leisurely pace. It was late afternoon and the trees seemed backlit, suffused with light.

"Do I like the park?" she asked.

He didn't want to lie to her, though God knew there had been lies between them before. "Almost everyone likes the park," he said.

"I was here as a child," she said. "Do you remember? The park was larger then."

He was thinking it was time to turn back, but he let the thought, with its disquieting urgencies, dissolve. They were getting along so well, he didn't want to disturb the rhythm that had brought them to this place.

They took the center path, but after a while it seemed more rewarding to take a right turn on a narrower, more cunning road, dotted at uncertain intervals with stone benches.

"Is this my warmest coat?" she asked him.

He took his coat off and put it around her shoulders. "Would you like to sit for a while?"

"If you do," she said. "I always ruin things for you."

"Isn't that the nature of marriage," he said.

They were between benches and he chose for their resting place the one they had already passed, shortening if not by much the distance necessary for return. As her bottom made acquaintance with the bench, she gave up a sigh, leaning into Josh to exclude the darkness. "I know what you're saying," she said. "You think I'm like my mother. It so happens I remember that we met in a park very much like this one. I was with another boy at the time, someone from my class…"

He continued to worry that they would not find their way back in the dark, but her story, which he had never heard before, fascinated him. He was desperate to hear how it turned out and he would sit there with her, he decided, shoulder to shoulder, as the temperature fell and the shadowy light went its vagrant way, to the bitter end.

THE STORY

He didn't know if he had read the story somewhere, in a magazine or book perhaps, or someone he didn't know very well, perhaps hardly knew at all, had told it to him at a party in an unguarded moment, or he had invented it himself some time ago and didn't know how to close it out so he had filed it away in his mind as something he might deal with in the future, when he had enough distance from it to contend with the material, or—the least likely of his alternatives—something like it had actually happened to him and, troubled by its implicit commentary, he had blocked it out and now, for its own reasons, it had returned to insist on itself, on its prerogative as narrative, its bloody need, its inalienable right, to have a life of its own separate from his uncertain connection to it, and what was he going to do about it, what could he do as a writer but honor its insistent presence by retelling the story in a way that would emphasize its uniqueness as an imaginative event while at the same time hoping that no one else after the fact would show up to make claim to it, which would mean that the story, for all its closeness to his heart—meaning his artistic vision—had never really been his in the first place and therefore what he had done with it would be vitiated by the charge of plagiarism laid at his door, rightful or not, and worse, make him regret his commitment to the story and even regret the story itself, which would be like falling out of love when he had announced to everyone that this one was forever, but then again no one, no one that counted, might show up to deny his right to the story when he had already made it his own, covering the traces of its origins in any event—but hadn't all stories, in a certain sense, been told before, which was the word on the media street, a popular conception or misconception and so irrelevant to his concerns at the moment (and damn it, where did the story come from anyway) which were (are) to produce a memorable version of the story, the best possible version given his gifts and limitations, whatever they may be, which is the business of others, critics and such, educated readers, to determine, his arrant immodesty best kept to himself far from the public eye or whatever goodwill his work has accrued over the years will leak through the holes in his reputation, which is a small thing as it is, with unspoken aspirations toward bettering its condition, and what did he really know what the general culture thought of his work if at all, did he even want to know…but let's get back to the story, he tells himself, it's the story that matters, he is only its executor, or caretaker perhaps, or parent, the one who keeps it clothed and fed until it is sufficiently formed to deal with the world without him around to mediate its existence, the story which concerns a writer not much like himself who has come into unspecified possession of a story of at once general interest and self-defining strangeness that seems to insist, virtually demand, that whoever takes it up give it voice, but as it has been entrusted to him, this extraordinary event, by whatever gods control the destinies of prose narrative (by chance, he supposed, and vision and luck), he feels burdened by such responsibility, perhaps even thwarted by it so it requires of him an act of will or presumption to give the story in question the kind of imaginative recreation it surely deserves and so the shadow of possible failure, possibly inevitable failure looms over his endeavor even as he feels he is solving whatever inherent mystery lies at its core, he is also falling short of the perfect accommodation of substance to form but no one will know while it remains in a state of ongoing inconclusion (in life, all stories go on indefinitely or slip away into ellipsis), so this sentence, which is the story, which embodies the story, cannot be allowed to, has to be held in abeyance as it acknowledges an implicit mortality wholly alien to the nature of perfection, achieve even the illusion of closure without permanently curtailing whatever hope for the earned unexpected it brings to the page, it cannot be brought to conclusion, it cannot be, it cannot, it...

TRAVELS WITH WIZARD

After turning sixty amid a debilitating winter that had hung on long beyond expectation, after his latest live-in girlfriend had elected to move on, after renewed feelings of hopelessness had moved in to replace her, the biographer Leo Dimoff, sensing the need for radical change in his life, decided to get a dog.

Why a dog?

For one thing, living alone after a lifelong failed apprenticeship in the relationship trade, Leo felt deprived, wanted companionship though without the attendant complications. All the women in his life, or so he understood his history of failures, had burdened him with unanswerable demands.

"You want a dog because they don't talk back," Sarah, his most recent former live-in companion, told him over dinner at the very Japanese restaurant that had hosted their breakup. They had lived together for almost a year in the not-so-distant, unremembered past and had remained contentious friends

"Dog owners are never called chauvinists," he said. "And certainly not by their dogs."

"I love dogs," she said, "though I've never had one. What kind of dog are you thinking of, Leo?"

"I've been doing the research," he said. "I may have read everything about choosing the right dog the written word had in stock. I may in fact have acquired more information than I know what to do with. What I'm in the market for is a medium-sized, aesthetically pleasing, low-maintenance puppy who is affectionate, intelligent, and, most importantly, faithful. I'd be grateful for suggestions."

"Whew!" she said, turning her face away to issue a brief, secretive smile. "Well, I know it's not for everyone, but I've always been partial to the Russell Terrier."

"I don't know," he said. "That's a kind of circus dog, isn't it? One of my dog texts—it may be *Puppies for Dummies*—says that Russells tend to be high-strung."

"Too high-strung, huh? You want a placid, doting, drooling dog, is that it? Mixed-breeds are thought to be less high-strung than full breeds, Leo. You could go to a shelter and pick out a puppy."

"I could," he said. "Would you accompany me?"

"I might," she said. "And then again I might not."

That the heart has its reasons and usually poor ones represented a good half of Leo's shaky acquired wisdom. On the other hand, as a biographer, he was generally esteemed for an empathic understanding of the wisdom and frailty of others.

Nevertheless, in careless love, he had come home one day with an odd-looking, long-legged, long-haired, big-nosed, tan and white puppy that had, said the shelter report, some lab, some poodle, and a soupçon of spaniel in its otherwise indecipherable makeup. The woman running the shelter, who reminded him of a former grade-school teacher whose name he sometimes remembered, said he could bring the puppy back in a week if it didn't work out. "It'll work out," he told her.

Leo stayed awake much of their first night together, concerned that the silent puppy, tentatively named Wizard after the subject of his latest biography, might suffocate without him there to monitor its sleep. The woman who ran the shelter had warned him that the infant dog, feeling displaced in new surroundings, might cry his first night away from the only home he knew. That Wizard's behavior defeated expectations gave the biographer, a worrier in the best of seasons, cause for concern. The puppy started the night on unselected pages of the *New York Times* at the foot of Leo's bed. In the morning, when Leo opened his eyes, unaware of having slept, his charge was on the pillow next to him. In fact it was Wizard's cry, or perhaps it was only a high-pitched bark, that woke Leo from a dream in which the small dog he was caring for grew unacceptably large overnight.

At Sarah's advice and against his own predilections, Leo took Wizard to a local trainer, a friend of Sarah's, also named Sara (without the h), for obedience lessons.

Rosy-cheeked, slightly pudgy, the trainer, the other Sara, seemed barely out of her teens. When Leo asked her age, all she would tell him was that she was older than she looked. And that she was very good at her job.

In the following moment, they had their second misunderstanding. It came when she asked him the puppy's name. "Wizard," he said, not yet comfortable with the choice.

"Whizzer?" she said.

"Wizard," he muttered.

"I understand," she said. "Whizzer."

From what he could tell, Wizard seemed to be failing his first lesson, which embarrassed the biographer who offered excuses for his charge's slow-wittedness. "He tends to be shy with strangers," Leo said.

"Oh, he's doing just fine," Sara said. "And since we're already friends—aren't we, Whizzer?" chucking the puppy under the chin, "—we can no longer be considered strangers. I think we need to do this twice a week and you need to practice commands with him in the morning before breakfast and at night before he goes to sleep. If it will make it easier for you, I'll come to your house next time."

Leo reluctantly accepted her offer, having no reason—none he could find words for—not to.

For the next several weeks, on Tuesdays and Fridays, Sara appeared at his door promptly at four thirty for Wizard's lesson. At their first session, Leo offered the trainer a cup of coffee, which she declined. Thereafter he made her herbal tea, specifically the ginseng-chai combination she favored, and more often than not the trainer stayed beyond the forty minutes set aside for the actual lesson. Though he was old enough to be her father and then some, Leo sometimes imagined that her extended stays had something to do with him.

"Whizzer's very bright," she told Leo, who, although pleased by the compliment, remained skeptical. Not only was the dog not toilet trained after three weeks in his care, but he tended to leave his shit just off the edge of the paper—usually the *NY Times* sports page—laid out to take its measure.

And then one day, when least expected, Wizard stopped doing his "business"—that repellent dog-manual euphemism—in inappropriate places. Not one to believe in undeserved good fortune, Leo obsessively searched the three rooms available to his charge, sometimes on hands and knees, before acknowledging that the puppy was not as dim as previously suspected.

Whenever Sara arrived—at times her knock at the door would be sufficient—Wizard would do a pirouette in ecstatic expectation, which made Leo jealous despite the murmurs of his better judgment. It was important of course that the puppy be fond of his trainer. Still, the 360-degree turn, sometimes restated, seemed a little much. Although Leo fed the puppy, doted on him, walked him in good and bad weather, early and late, he sometimes imagined that Wizard, in his faithless heart, actually preferred Sara.

So after a while, after a particularly good training session, after herbal tea and cookies, Leo wondered aloud if Wizard (and owner) weren't sufficiently trained at this point to go it on their own.

"If that's what you want," she said, her stern, cherubic face in unacknowledged collapse. "He still has a few things to learn, you know. You said he pulls on the leash when he sees another dog. We might do a few outdoor lessons. It's much harder to get him to obey when there are distractions around."

It struck Leo that Sara, though otherwise a bundle of positive qualities, had almost no sense of humor. Possibly her sense of humor was so subtle that his own crude radar failed to acknowledge it.

"You've done very well with him," Leo said, trying not to sound condescending. "We're both pleased, you know, with his considerable progress."

His compliment seemed to distress her. "If there's a financial burden," she said, "I'd be willing to cut my fee. Would that make a difference? I think Whizzer is on the verge of his next big breakthrough."

"Look, why don't we take next week off," Leo said, "as a kind of vacation for all of us. I'm doing a reading from my book on Nikola Tesla in Rochester and I'm thinking of taking Wizard with me to see how he handles the trip."

"I have a sister who lives in Rochester," Sara said.

"Do you?"

"Yes, and she's been having a hard time since her divorce. I've been planning to go up and see her, but then something always comes up that gets in the way. I'll have to check my schedule, but maybe I could go along for the ride and give you both a hand. Have you considered what you're going to do with the pup when you're reading whatever it is in front of an audience?"

Feeling trapped, Leo improvised a barely credible explanation as to why it wouldn't work for Sara to accompany him. "I appreciate your offer," he added.

"I'd better go," Sara said.

Leo awakes the next morning aware that it was a mistake to reject Sara's offer, a foolish and mean-spirited miscalculation. Perhaps the only way out for him is to phone the trainer, apologize for his abruptness, admit that he needs her on the trip and ask her, virtually plead with her, to join them. He has allowed himself to imagine Sara's pleasure in getting this call from him.

"You're too late," she says. "I've already made other plans."

That is the not the answer he has anticipated, so he hangs on waiting hopelessly for better news.

"Is there something else?" she asks.

"That's about it," he says, noting out of the corner of his eye that Wizard has one of his shoes in his mouth, wagging his head ferociously from side to side as if it were a fearsome opponent.

"Stop that," he calls to the dog.

"What are you saying?" Sara says. "What should I stop?"

"Not you. Wizard was chewing on one of my shoes."

"Whatever," she says. "You never shout at your dog. If he's well-trained, a quiet command should be sufficient to deter him. I should think you would know that by now."

"It's only in the last few days that he's started these life-and-death battles with my shoes. He gets so much pleasure out of it, it seems churlish of me to deny him."

"I don't know that you want to encourage bad behavior, do you? If it were me, I wouldn't want him chewing on my shoes."

"Of course you're right," he says.

2

There are a few timid, out-of-season snow flurries when they take off in the morning for Rochester, but several hours into the journey, Leo finds himself driving in blizzard conditions. Losing traction here and there despite his all-wheel-drive Forester, he considers pulling over to the side of the road to wait out the worst of the storm. That the others seem oblivious to any danger makes it difficult for him to concede to the weather. Wizard, trussed into the passenger seat next to him, is staring out the window like a tourist. Sara, keeping company in the backseat with her cell phone, has been trying relentlessly to reach her sister in Rochester, the phone failing or the sister not available, Sara unnervingly patient.

After a while Sara gets through to her sister and Leo learns that the reading has been postponed. Exhausted from his unrewarded efforts, he suggests they stop at the Wanderer's Motel in the near distance while waiting for the storm to abate. As they have no plans to stay the night, they agree for economy's sake to take a single cabin. So as not to set off any alarms, Leo registers Sara as his wife.

"You must be exhausted," Sara says as they move through the mix of sleet and rain to their cabin. "Why don't you sack out and I'll get the pup from the car and give him his bathroom walk."

"That's okay" he says. "I appreciate the offer. It's just that walking Wizard is one of the unsung highlights of my day."

"Oh go ahead, you look dead on your feet. I know how stressful it can be driving in treacherous weather, Leo. You don't have to prove anything to me."

So, feeling anything but grateful, carrying an overnight case in each hand, Leo lets himself into the motel room while Sara takes the puppy on the stretch leash, the two wandering into the distance like snow ghosts. The boxy cabin is furnished, along with a low-slung three-drawer dresser, by a writing table with a Bible wrapped in plastic and two picture postcards on its otherwise bare surface, with two three-quarter-size beds barely a foot apart. Not bothering to remove his shoes, Leo throws himself on the bed farthest from the door.

He dozes or imagines he has and wakes to find himself still alone in the room. Where are the others?

There is a heavy green curtain over what seems like a back window and, though it takes a while, he finally locates a device that parts the brocaded cloth.

He is surprised to discover a back garden with tables under umbrellas—a place to picnic, perhaps—overwhelmed by the blinding whiteness of the still falling sleet. He has no idea what he is looking for, but as his eyes adjust, he sees something that speaks to the worst of his expectations.

He closes his eyes as if to return to a dream from which he then might shake himself awake. When, after a moment of inconsequential reverie, he allows his eyes to open, nothing has changed or nothing has changed sufficiently to put his original perception in doubt.

As near as he can make out, Sara is sitting under one of the umbrellas in the garden with her back to him. At first he assumes that she has returned Wizard to the car, but then he sees that she is not alone. Something—a head, Wizard's head most likely—is sticking out from the opening in her yellow down jacket and Sara's hooded head is tilted forward so that the two heads seem at some point to converge. It is only when she returns to her original position that Leo can tell that Sara and Wizard have been—there is no other word to describe it—kissing. Sara's head moves forward again and her mouth meets the dog's (a suspicion of tongue flashing), which is more than Leo can bear to watch.

Not wanting to eavesdrop any longer than he has, he closes the curtain and goes into the bathroom to see if he recognizes the face in the mirror over the sink that answers his troubled glance.

Perhaps ten minutes later, Sara enters the room alone, reporting that she has left the dog in the car because of the NO PETS ALLOWED sign they hadn't noticed before.

"Did you get some sleep?" she asks, pulling off her boots. "I stayed out for a while so as not to wake you."

Lying on her back, eyes flickering shut, the whisper of a snore complicating the indeterminate hum of the room, the trainer is apparently asleep before Leo can frame an answer to her question.

A few hours later, the weather has quieted sufficiently for them to return to the road. Unaccompanied in front this time around—Sara and Wizard shoulder to shoulder in the backseat—Leo feels deserted. A sadness he hasn't acknowledged in months, perhaps since the dog entered his life, holds him in its sway.

Could they have missed a turn? They have been driving a while now—he has lost track of the time—and the passing scene, what he can make of it from the badly lit road he has been following slavishly, seems unfamiliar.

"Are we lost?" Sara asks him.

"I don't see how," he says. "We haven't left the route we started on."

"Whizzer is getting anxious," she says. "He senses something's wrong."

They are approaching a restaurant called The Helden Inn on their right and Leo announces, as if he were some kind of tour guide, that it might be a good idea to stop for a bite. "What do you think?" he says to no one in particular.

"If that's what you want to do," Sara says. "I can't speak for everyone, but I suspect we're all a bit peckish."

There are an impressive number of vehicles, mostly high-end SUVs, in the restaurant lot, which suggests, given the deterrence of the weather, a devoted local following. "I think we may have lucked out," he says to Sara.

Sara calls his attention to a sign on the parking lot side of the inn rising out of the white ground, which offers the modest recommendation, "JUST GOOD FOOD," the remark in quotes, the speaker unattributed. Underneath the quote, in smaller letters, it says, PETS AND CHILDREN WELCOME.

Leo parks the Forester at the far end of the lot—he feels fortunate to find a space in the crowd of vehicles—and they have to wade, Wizard in Sara's arms, through several inches of slush to reach the inn.

As they find their way inside, an elderly couple, oddly costumed (the old man in lederhosen, the woman in frilly blouse and apron), seem to be waiting for them (or someone) in the cavernous foyer. "Do you have reservations?" the woman asks, her broad smile welcoming them.

"We don't," Leo says. "Is that a problem?"

"There are only problems if we make them problems," the woman says, her accent vaguely foreign, the smile seemingly frozen on her face. "We'll do our best to take care of you. Please to follow."

She leads them into a spacious dining room—thirteen tables, by Leo's quick count—in which surprisingly there is only one other diner, a fat man in a three-piece suit, at the far side of the room, working at what appears to be an elaborate cream-filled desert.

Leo dries Wizard off with his rumpled cloth napkin while Sara inspects her menu. "There isn't anything here I can eat," she says. "I don't eat meat."

"What about a salad?" Leo says. "They must have salads."

"The truth is," Sara says, "and I hope you won't mention this to anyone, though I don't eat meat, I don't really like salads."

Wizard, who seems to have grown during the difficult trip, barks from under the table at some unseen menace.

The proprietress, her perpetual smile a kind of rictus, returns with a basket of sliced rye bread and three glasses of water. She seems poised to take their order when someone or something whistles from the kitchen and she hurries off.

Coming out from under the table, Wizard has taken residence on one of the padded chairs, accomplishing the feat with an impressive jump.

The fat man on the other side of the room lifts his head languorously from his dessert long enough to clap.

When Leo has a chance to go through the menu, which is several pages long, he has a greater appreciation of Sara's concern. The Helden Inn is celebrating something called Carnivore Days and all or virtually all of the dishes offered have some kind of animal meat as their base. Even under "Starters." Leo can find nothing that seems like a green salad. Under the Carnivore Days Specials, there is a quote in italics as a kind of epigraph.

"The carnivore loves his animals so much
he is willing to eat them."

—*The Management*

"If you don't want to stay," he whispers to Sara, who has been negotiating a slice of stale bread, "I'm willing to leave."

His offer seems in equal measure to puzzle and please her. "Leo, wouldn't it be rude to just walk out after they've gone to all this trouble on our behalf? I was actually thinking of ordering my first burger in about six years. Did you notice that they have a puma burger on the menu?" She smiles self-deprecatingly, almost seductively. "I've been known to compromise in emergencies."

Out of the corner of his eye, he notices that the suited fat man has fallen asleep face down in his desert. Sara, intent on the menu's extended narrative, seems not to notice.

An odd muffled cry sounds from behind one of the walls.

Wondering, not for the first time, where the people from the parked cars have gone, Leo takes a $20 bill from his wallet and leaves it under the matching white enamel salt and pepper shakers. "That should pay for the service," he says. "Did you notice that they actually have a 'Bow Wow Burger' on the menu?"

"They don't?" she says, rising from her chair.

Sara is in the process of putting the puppy under her jacket when the proprietress, her smile unaltered, returns with a tray of unidentifiable appetizers. "I apologize for the delay," she says. "The help isn't always what you want."

Leo is about to offer an explanation for their abrupt departure, but instead takes Sara's hand and heads to the door that leads to the cavernous foyer.

The old man in the lederhosen is standing by the register as they hurry past him. "Come visit us again," he says in an uninflected voice. "And don't forget to drive safely."

Since almost all the vehicles in the lot are covered with some residue of the weather, it is hard to determine in the dark which car is theirs. In his hurry to get going, Leo, using the sleeve of his coat, clears off the front window of the wrong Forester.

A Lexus SUV, pulling out from the row behind them, startles them with its horn. The driver, who could be the younger sister of the proprietress, rolls down a window and offers them a ride.

In the chaos of the moment, Leo is tempted to accept, but Sara, who is clearing off another car, says, "Wait a second. I think I found ours."

They pile into the Forester Sara has cleared, though Leo is not at all sure it is the one that had brought them there.

This time, Sara drives while Leo and Wizard sit next to each other in the back, a larger space between them than the one Leo observed between Sara and the puppy when he was at the wheel. Still he is pleased to be alone with his charge without other responsibilities, and he reaches out awkwardly to rub the puppy's head. Closing his eyes, Wizard accepts Leo's homage. When after a while Leo reclaims his hand, Wizard turns to look at him, the dog's wise face making unspoken judgments, seeing through to the very bottom of the biographer.

For an unguarded moment, Leo considers apologizing for his failings, promising to do his best to transcend his limitations in the future.

At some point, at Leo's request—the gauge registering empty— Sara pulls into a Mobil station to gas up and to find out where they might be in relation to where they are going. Apparently, they have been heading for the most part in the wrong direction and are farther away from home than ever. The source of their information, an overeager teenaged attendant, says he knows a shortcut and he draws them a not-quite-decipherable map on a coffee-stained napkin.

"What do you want to do?" Sara asks Leo, showing him the makeshift map. "We could stop at the motel we just passed and start out fresh in the morning, or we could turn around and drive through the night."

Instinctively, he turns to Wizard, but the shaggy dog, head pressed against Leo's leg, eyes mostly shut, offers merely the example of his silence.

As Leo considers his options, he imagines them—Sara driving, himself in back with Wizard—moving on in whatever direction, letting the trip take them where it will, the hand-drawn map, the various maps just an excuse to pursue space and distance.

At some point, Sara pulls the car off to the side of the road. "I'm getting tired," she says, moving into the backseat, occupying Wizard's other side. "Would you take over?"

"Take over?" Leo has his arm around Wizard's shoulder.

"Yes, would you mind taking the next stretch?"

"I don't mind," he says, imagining himself getting out of the car and taking his place behind the wheel while in fact not moving at all.

"I'm glad you don't mind," she says, putting an arm around Wizard from the other side, grazing Leo's fingers.

The trip continues a while without calculable movement, the passengers in the backseat each with an arm around Wizard, hugging each other through the surrogate in their midst.

THE READING

The poet B travels by train to give a reading of his poems at an obscure liberal arts college in southern Pennsylvania. His lime-green Saab, which has been virtually the shell on his back, has come down with a case of transmission failure the morning of the trip. Worse news, it is his habit to believe, lies ahead. When his wife left him nineteen days ago to run off with a criminal lawyer, his life, which had been finely tuned for years, fell abruptly and perhaps irremediably into screeching disarray.

The train ride is uneventful, a slideshow of undeveloped pictures. B uses the time to read and to muse on the disrepair of his life. When the train arrives at the college station twenty minutes late, no one is on the platform to meet him. What's that all about? Already nightfall, the dark platform seems a deserted street in the middle of nowhere. Has he been lured here only to be abandoned in darkness? The tips of B's fingers are chilled, almost numb from the cold. He paces the platform, his hands in the pockets of his leather jacket, and waits. It is unrewarding activity, pacing and waiting, reminding him of the bad luck he is embarrassed to believe in and can't seem to shake.

He approaches the grizzled ticket-seller, who withholds speech as if there were no getting it back once given away. Still, if you ask the right questions, he has always believed, the information you're after will work its way through the cracks. The college, he interpolates from the ticket-seller's grunts and headshakes, is too far away to walk. There are no cabs available after six thirty. The station's two public phones have been out of order for months. After a while another train arrives. B, who has nothing better to do, meets it as if he were meeting himself. Two people get off at the dark and deserted station. One is a woman he knows slightly, a poet he met two years ago at a writer's conference and fell in love with at sight. He has not seen her since.

When he introduces himself (she doesn't remember having met him), the woman, Y, assumes B is a representative of the college there to meet her, a delusion she holds onto even after he explains that he too has been stood up. When he tells her of their mutual predicament, she reproaches him in a graceful way on his failures as a host. "You must learn to plan ahead," she says. "Not everything we do works out as we intend it." He acknowledges the wisdom of her remarks, suggests they walk toward the college with the hope of promoting a ride along the way. She will stay at the station, she says, and wait for them to come to her. It is her method in all things to let others come to her.

What can B do but wait with her. "I can't leave you," he says, a remark which earns him a hit-and-run kiss on the cheek.

"Never?" she asks.

He wonders at that moment if there weren't something fateful about them meeting this way, at the deserted college station. "It does stand to reason, doesn't it?" B says. "That the college, having planned on our being there, will send someone to claim us." The remark earns him a second kiss, this one passed from her fingers to his cheek.

They sit for a while on one of the dark platform's two backless stone benches, leaning into each other to keep the cold wind from taking residence between them. "I do remember you now," she says. They talk about walking up and down to get warm or going inside the building to escape the wind. Ways of warming themselves is not their only subject. He is surprised when he puts his arm around her and she cuddles into his shoulder, as much surprised at his own gesture as at hers. His lost and barely remembered feelings for this woman revisit uninvited. Sensation returns to the tips of his fingers.

When they stand up to go inside, she lets herself be kissed. She covers his mouth with her hand when he tries or seems about to try to explain himself. It is not as if he had anything to say that had not been heard.

It is uncomfortable inside the small waiting room, airless and overbright, radiators wheezing like slumbering drunks. In the light, he discovers that she is not the person he thought she was, not the one he fell in love with at sight. This unlooked-for discovery leaves him emotionally bereft, as if his most passionate feelings had remained on the platform without him.

He doesn't tell her that she is the wrong one. They sit like strangers now, slightly apart, each reading a book of the other's poems. The taste of her tongue, the weight of her head on his shoulder, are barely a memory. And this is the way they are, lost and found, when the awkwardly shy assistant professor who had been sent to pick them up makes his apologetic appearance. "Can you believe I couldn't find the station?" he tells them.

The assistant professor drives them toward the college in his cluttered brown and green station wagon, the seats and floor decorated with debris, old newspapers and magazines, loose Pampers, broken plastic toys, almost every surface occupied. They run out of gas before they arrive and their surrogate host, who is prepared for such emergencies, hurries off with a one-gallon can under his arm, telling them not to worry, that he's done this before.

Moments after he leaves, a white, late-model oversized American car drives up alongside their beached whale. A white-haired man in formal clothes, a trustee perhaps, sticks his head out the window and asks them if they would like a ride to the college. B, who has no trust in the assistant professor, accepts immediately (though his door won't open), but the woman in back (the one he's fallen in and out of love with in the past hour) says the appropriate thing to do would be to wait for their driver to return. B argues his case, but the woman won't be dissuaded from what she knows to be the right course. "I can't leave her," he explains to the trustee, who drives off without them.

"When you say that," she tells him when they're alone again, "it makes me want to cry."

The assistant professor returns, feeds the empty tank, starts the car, and they drive to the college without further mishap. Except they arrive on campus ten minutes after the reading is scheduled and they find themselves locked out of the appointed building, Affect Hall. What's with this college? Even if they get the building open (and the assistant professor has, with that intent in mind, gone off to find a key), where will an audience come from? There is no one else, no small clique of English majors, waiting to get in. At that point, B realizes that he has left his overnight bag at the train station. The only thing he can do, which is of little practical value, is imagine himself calling the station and asking the uncommunicative ticket-seller to put his bag in a safe place for him until he can manage his return.

A security guard unlocks the building from inside. Momentarily, they are milling around in a small auditorium, the other poet, Y, holding his hand in a secretive way. An audience of five assembles itself. The poet asks his companion whether she'd like to go first or second. She has been drinking from a flask and is slightly befuddled. "What are my other choices?" she asks.

The chairman of the English department, who wears black glass-es, arrives to introduce the readers, or so B understands the man's role when he takes the podium. The chairman, who is blind, reads his prepared text with his fingers. His written introduction seems for the first ten minutes or so elaborate and obscure. Neither B nor the faded beauty Y is mentioned by name. What's it all about? The blind chairman goes on and on as if it were not an introduction at all but a paper elaborating a theory of language. "Language is the whim of silence," says the speaker.

Panic moves B to get up from his seat in the front row and look around the room. Are the others in the audience as astonished at the blind chairman's performance as he is? "Sit down," Y whispers at him. "Don't you find this strange?" he asks her. She puts a finger over her lips, splitting a smile. When he sits down, she puts her lips over his to preserve his unhappy silence.

When the introduction goes into its second hour most of the small audience leaves. Only B and Y and the chairman's hearing-impaired wife continue their vigil.

The assistant professor comes running down the aisle, waving his arms. What's the problem? "There's been a mix-up," he says. "The Broadsnore Lecture is in here. You people are supposed to be in another room altogether."

Y insists on staying to the end of the lecture and B is conflicted on whether to leave or not. "Come with me," he pleads.

"It's not right to walk out on him," she says.

B follows the assistant professor into a somewhat smaller room down the hall. There is an overflow crowd, as it turns out, waiting for him. They stamp their feet in welcome on his appearance at the podium. "You can't believe what I went through to get here," he says. That brings a laugh.

It falls to the assistant professor to introduce him. "I don't have to tell you how privileged we are to have this man with us today," he starts out, an inappropriate remark that speaks to B's unacknowledged secret self. The fulsome introduction continues. B is pictured as a defender of the defenseless, a man willing to take up causes so unpopular no one else in his right mind would dare touch them. What's going on? The praise touches him almost to the point of tears. How does this bumptious assistant professor know so much about him, he wonders. It is as if he were introducing some figure of national prominence and not a relatively obscure poet known, if at all, for his uncompromising difficulty.

And then his name is mentioned (though it is not exactly his name) to standing applause. He has been mistaken for someone else, a trial lawyer (and former basketball great) who has a predilection for representing only the blatantly guilty. At first B plans to deny that he is the famous lawyer they've been waiting for, but then he thinks, Well, maybe there's a more graceful way to avoid the embarrassment of this foolish mistake. Besides, he has never had a crowd this large come to hear him. An ambiguous disclaimer might be sufficient. "I am not the man you think I am," he says, which invites further applause. "Your support and affection have made this moment possible. There can be no justice without a constituency that acknowledges the possibility of justice." Having run out of platitudes, he waits for inspiration.

"Why do I do what I do?" he asks. The answer sits waiting for him. "Because if I don't, no one else will." The audience offers him a standing ovation. The back door opens and Y, looking tired and lost, slips into the room. "To give you a sense of who I am," he says, "I want to read you some poems by a poet who I sometimes think speaks for me." The audience clears its collective throat. Y alone applauds.

B reads his poems for twenty minutes to mumbled confusion. The audience has a glazed look on its collective face when he stops. "Are there any questions?" he asks.

An older woman in the third row has her hand up in a determined way and he nods in her direction. She turns to look behind her before speaking. "I don't normally ask questions in public," she says in a histrionic voice. "This is what I want to know. Would you defend someone who would kill his own mother?"

"If I don't, who will?" he says. "Next question."

"If you didn't, another headline-seeker would," a voice shouts out.

B points to a young girl in the back. "In your opinion, what is the worst crime a person could commit?" she asks in a quivering voice. "And would you defend such a person?"

B repeats the question for those of the audience who might not have heard it. "The worst crime, huh? The worst crime is the betrayal of self. The worst crime is the betrayal of love. The worst crime is any crime that has a victim. Such crimes are unforgivable and must be defended."

"Yeah," the audience chants in one voice.

A middle-aged man with alcoholic's eyes asks, "Have you ever committed an unforgivable crime yourself?"

"Yes," says B.

"Are you willing to say what that crime was?"

"No, I'm not."

"Animals have rights too," a woman in the fifth row says in an angry voice. "Do you think the killing of an innocent animal should be a capital offense? I want a yes or no answer."

"Yes or no," says B, playing for the easy laugh. "Depends on how innocent the animal is."

The animal woman gets up and walks out of the room in an earnest huff. Her departure, or perhaps B's answer, freezes the crowd. B waits patiently for another hand to rise. Y has the next question.

"Were the poems you read," she asks, "written by one of your unforgivable clients?"

"We are all forgivable, I hope," says B.

The assistant professor ends the question period by stepping in front of B and inviting everyone to a reception in a lounge downstairs—wine without chemical additives and low-fat cheese—where the audience will be given opportunity to meet face to face with their celebrated guest.

B, weary of the imposture, looks for a way out, takes Y's hand and pulls her inside a stairwell away from the crowd.

"What do you say we pursue justice elsewhere," he says. He expects resistance and is almost disappointed when she says, "Where can we go?"

"Let's just wait here until the crowd disperses," he says, realizing in the next moment that it is not Y whose hand he has taken but someone else, the woman who had been standing next to Y, the one concerned with meting out justice to animal slayers.

Y finds him with the animal woman before B can excuse himself to leave. She calls him by his presumed name, tells him (eyeing the other woman) that his fans are waiting for him in the lounge.

What fans are those? B makes a whirlwind tour of the lounge, pressing flesh like a politician, dispensing whatever wisdom the oiled tongue has to offer.

After the reception there is another party, then dinner, then another party. Between the first and third party he has lost Y with whom he has again fallen in love. Anyway it is late and he is slightly drunk and very tired so he goes to the room they've assigned him in the Alumni House to take a nap or bed down for the night, however it goes.

When he opens the door to the room he assumes is his, Room 2 according to the number on his key, he senses that something is amiss. Though the lock on the door answers to his key, there is an intruder in the bed sleeping soundlessly. It is the second thing he notices, the impostor in his bed; the first is the neatly folded pile of clothes on the chair across the room. B leaves silently, takes his outrage and exhaustion with him, sits on the stairs in the hall with his head in his hands. What can he do? He gets a brainstorm, decides to try the doors to the other rooms. There is a couple in Room 1 fucking in a dispirited way and B's head is in and out before the couple, who turn to stare at him, have time to ask him what he wants. Room 3 resists his key. Room 4, his last hope for sanctuary, is unlocked and unoccupied. B slips into the room like a thief.

He locks the door, pulls off his shoes without undoing the laces, and falls into bed—perhaps even falls asleep. Next thing he knows, someone is knocking on the door. Then he hears a key in the lock and the door click open. A man with a cane walks haltingly toward the bed. The figure takes off its clothes, piles them neatly on the floor, and slides under the covers next to him.

"There's someone here," B says in a choked voice. The intruder raises his head, looks directly at B—their faces are no more than six inches apart—but seems not to see him. The man is asleep and snoring softly before B can protest again. He imagines himself climbing out of bed and reclaiming his shoes, a gesture he repeats over and over again, waking hours later from this dream to find a heavy arm sprawled possessively across his chest.

B slips off the bed, searches the floor for his shoes, escapes the room on his hands and knees. Y is in the hall, standing with her back to him, smoking a cigarette.

"You missed a great party," she says when he touches her shoulder. When she turns he notices an ugly purple bruise under her right eye.

"What happened?" he asks her.

"Nothing," she says, averting her eyes. "Nothing worth talking about." She takes a pair of sunglasses from her purse and puts them on.

"Did they give you a room?" he asks.

"Better than that," she says. "I have the keys to a station wagon parked outside that we can take to the station. The thing is, I can't leave with you…and don't say what I think you're going to say."

"I'll wait until you're ready to leave," he says.

"Look, it's a long story," Y says, "but I promised to stay with the assistant professor, just until he gets on his feet. His wife and children left him nine days ago and he's in a bad state, suicidal, needy and potentially violent."

The news troubles B but he says nothing more about it, waits his occasion.

In the car, in the passenger seat, just as Y is about to start the engine, he has an urge to put his head in her lap, which is what he does. They kiss twice before moving to the back of the station wagon. "You never said anything," she says.

It is morning, the back door of the wagon is opened. The sudden light disturbs their sleep, discovers them in disarray, B's pants bunched at the ankles, Y's bra perched on a stack of *American Scholar* magazines like a huddled bird. A small crowd of onlookers makes its presence felt.

After that, the despondent assistant professor, full of mock bravado, traces of tears glazing his glasses, drives them to the station.

"I can't leave him like this," Y says to B when they park.

Leave him, B wants to say, but instead leaves the arena of the car himself. "I'll wait for you inside the station," he says to Y. She nods to him in uncommitted acknowledgment.

He discovers his overnight case sitting in the waiting room and he picks it up and puts it on his lap, reclaims his former life.

According to the schedule in his jacket pocket the next train for New York City comes and goes in nine minutes. The one after that is three hours and twenty minutes down the road.

Five minutes pass and Y is still in the station wagon, locked in conversation with the aggrieved assistant professor. B worries that Y won't get back in time to make the train. When he looks over his shoulder to see if Y is on her way, the brown and green wagon is no longer on vigil outside. B rushes out to look for Y just as he hears the train huffing carelessly toward the station. Y's undeniable absence echoes through the parking lot. He has lost her again. It is always the case with him: every loss seems the same loss, the first loss, the only loss.

B rushes back to board the train, unaware in his haste that the train he boards is actually coming from where he means to go.

B is dozing at a window seat, unaware that he is heading toward Ohio and points west, when someone slides lightly into the seat next to him. Her perfume is familiar; so is the feel of her arm on his shoulder. "You left without me," she whispers, "after all your promises. That's hard to forgive." She presents him with a ghostly peck on the cheek, the bare touch of her lips.

The opening phrase of a poem forms itself in his mind.

I sensed the sky closing like the door of an abandoned...

He acknowledges her reproach with a nod and closes his eyes to the unfamiliar countryside at the window—a field of motionless brown and white cows with a ramshackle red barn in the distance, a landscape absent from his history until this moment—now edging irreversibly away into the past.

Will she be there, he wonders, when in the course of things he finds the will or the courage or whatever it takes to look back?

SHAPESHIFTING

We had always considered Joel crazy, but not, if you will, crazy crazy. There is a difference. For Joel, who had exhibitionist impulses, craziness was a form of self-presentation. He was a character in search of an audience, a shy provocateur with an over-the-top, uncensored imagination. If it was his way to see conspiracy in virtually every public event; there was something in his manner, a sly, self-amused half-smile, that suggested a barely hidden ironic subtext. As it suited me to believe, Joel knew, or some part of him knew, that his outrageous scenarios had only metaphoric counterpart in the real world. Match that with the evidence of his private life. Married with two grown daughters (never divorced, like most of the rest of us), a successful ad company exec, he seemed, on balance, at least as together as most.

As Joel got older, however, the line between performer and performance became harder to distinguish. And then just recently, his wife, Dotty, confided to Helena, my live-in girlfriend, that Joel was behaving oddly, which worried her. What I said when she passed on Dotty's remark to me was, "How could she tell?" I was kidding, of course, but all jokes have their own hidden truths.

It all started, or seemed to, about a year or so after the Kennedy assassination. At a dinner party at the home of mutual friends, in

which fewer than half of those present thought Oswald the lone as-
sassin, Joel offered an elaborate scenario for the Kennedy shooting,
which included a network of secret doubles, two Rubys, two Os-
walds, and—I've heard this nowhere else—two Kennedys.

"Two Kennedys, huh? What about two Johnsons?" I asked.

"No," he answered with deadpan solemnity and perfect comic
timing, "one Johnson was more than enough."

And then there was the election year when he announced that
the two major parties were in collusion and had decided between
them in secret meetings who would be the winner this time around.
It was either his reason for not voting—I forget now—or for sup-
porting a third-party candidate who was destined to end up with no
electoral votes. I was not alone in pointing out to him the high level
of hostility between the two parties, the unforgivable things spokes-
men of one party said about candidates of the other. How did that
jibe with his theory? He would wink and say, "Well, they have to
make it look good, don't they?" And then he would offer us a drink
(or not) and talk about something else, something closer to home.
He rarely elaborated on his theories, presuming, or so his manner
suggested, that his perceptions were self-evident to anyone who had
his wits about him.

To tell the truth, some of his pronouncements had for fleeting
moments crossed my mind as well, only to be dispelled by rational
second thoughts.

"So what is it this time?" I pressed Helena, who had been grudging about passing on the details of Dotty's confidence. Helena and
Dotty had been roommates at Wellesley and were exceedingly, sometimes vexingly, close. Still, it was Dotty I had to thank for Helena—
she and Joel had, rather cunningly I have to say, arranged for us to
meet.

"He accused Dotty of being an imposter," she said. "Stuff like that."

"He was speaking metaphorically, I assume."

"Dotty doesn't think so. He told her that he found her imposture—that was the word he used, imposture—sympathetic, even liked her at times better than the original, whom he nevertheless missed. That's terrible. Don't you think that's terrible?"

I nodded dutifully, more amused than horrified, but I continued to believe, or wanted to believe, that Joel was not exactly saying what he seemed to be saying. "So what did she say in response?"

"What would anyone say? After she cried for a couple of hours, she asked him to get help or to move out. He said he'd rather give up his home than put himself in the hands of some overpriced fraud."

"She asked him to move out?" I had trouble connecting the dots.

"What did I just say?"

"They've been together for close to—what?—thirty-five years. She knows what he's like. This can't have been as big a surprise to her as she's making out."

"Excuse me," Helena said. "Conjecturing a John F. Kennedy double is very different from telling the person you've lived with for thirty-three years that she's an imposter."

"I take your point," I said. Unlike Joel, my usual mode was not to provoke disputes, but on the contrary I was known—it was my self-presentation—to go out of my way to keep the peace. "He didn't actually move out, did he?"

"No," she conceded, "though nothing has been resolved. As a matter of fact, Dotty wondered if you would be willing to talk to Joel."

"Do I have to?" I said. "About what? You really want me to ask him if he thinks Dotty is not herself? Joel and I have never discussed our private lives."

"I told her you would do it," she said.

2

Though neither of us were drinkers, at least not anymore, we met at a downtown bar for our talk—I was hoping Joel would find a way to say no when I suggested it, but he accepted as soon as the invitation was in the air. It was almost as if he had been anticipating the request. He arrived late, late enough for me to think he wasn't coming, and seemed at least at the outset uncharacteristically subdued.

"I know what you're going to say," Joel said after we had ordered our second beers and the small talk had shrunk to the point of near invisibility.

"Yeah," I said. "I thought you might."

And then for close to an hour, with a few momentary stops for breath, he talked non-stop, his subject transforming almost with every sentence, telling me more than I wanted to hear—it was like being trapped inside a buzz saw—and not a lot that I wanted to know.

I'd like to cut away from this scene for the moment to one that followed after I returned home and gave Helena a generalized report of our inconclusive meeting.

"He must have said more than that," she said. "You were with him for hours."

"It was as if he were talking in tongues," I said. "Some of it made a kind of sense, but there was not much connective thread."

"Does he really believe Dotty is an imposter?"

"I don't think the subject came up. It may have, but it went by so quickly, I can't remember the implication."

"Sometimes you have to ask these things," she said. "You didn't find out anything, did you? Nothing. Nada. Zip."

"If that's what you want to believe," I said.

"I have to tell Dotty something. I bragged that you were good at getting information from people who didn't naturally confide. But you struck out this time, didn't you? What am I going to tell Dotty?"

"You could tell her that I struck out."

She left the room, which was the kitchen, but returned momentarily. "Why do I feel that there's something you're not telling me? It feels to me that it's the guys against the women, which is not like you. I wish you would tell me that I've gotten it wrong."

"What I'm going to tell you now, Josh," he said, "I'm sure you already know, though perhaps you haven't formulated it for yourself quite the way I have. We all suspected when the movie, the original *Invasion of the Body Snatchers*, appeared that there were aspects of its story that seemed closer to prescience than fantasy. Isn't that so?" I nodded when he paused for an answer. "Well, maybe fifteen years ago, maybe twenty-five, maybe thirty, maybe even longer than that, an advance party of what I call shape-shifting extraterrestrials took residence in the United States. They were here whenever it was they arrived mainly for observation and study and they kept a relatively low profile. Only rarely, perhaps out of boredom or whatever, did they intrude on our everyday lives. Gradually, and I have some theories as to why which are probably obvious to you, their mission became more aggressive. As shapeshifters, they had the capacity to replicate any living form and they decided, or their high command decided, to probe our civilization. Who knew what their intention was beyond mischief or malice or some kind of godlike vengeance. We're talking about a civilization so advanced that its way of perceiving was probably beyond our power even to imagine. You may remember that after the World Trade Center tragedy, I said it was likely that there was more to that than meets the eye." I did remember and I reluctantly said, "Uh-huh."

"It's clear to me now that there were no suicide bombers as such. Or that at least half of the hijacking crew (as well as their organizers) were shape-shifting extraterrestrials, and when the planes exploded they didn't die, at least not in the sense that we understand death, but merely lost their human shapes or exchanged them for new ones. At the same time, these outsiders, these uninvited visitors as I call them, had infiltrated our government at its highest echelon. I can't say for sure who is and who isn't at this juncture, though I have my suspicions and, as we've seen, they initiated actions designed to undermine the prestige and power of what had been the most prestigious and powerful nation in our world. The seemingly pointless war in Iraq, to be understood, has to be seen as a hideous extraterrestrial amusement. They're fucking with us, buddy. You can see that, can't you?"

"I don't know, Joel," I said in a small voice, cowed by his certainty. "There are also other explanations."

"Okay. Okay," he said impatiently. "There is always some half-credible official explanation for whatever. Believe what you like if it gives you comfort. But you can see from the people around you, can't you, that the shapeshifters have taken over more than just the leading players on the big stage. As with all public disasters, this one has its private ramifications."

There seemed no point in arguing with him. "All right," I said. "Say I accept your explanations, what's next? What can I do that would help the situation?"

"I've given that a lot of thought," he said. "There's nothing we can do, Josh, nothing that would alter things, beyond helping those in the dark see the situation for what it is. I've told you what I know at great personal risk in the hope that you'll pass it on to others. It's a start, an inescapable necessity, to have an awareness of what you're up against. You see that, don't you? I'm trying to be hopeful, I really am, but my gut feeling tells me there is no hope. Or very, very little.

Our only hope, as I reckon it, and that's a huge stretch, is that the shapeshifters will get bored with their manipulations and go away."
He looked as if he were doing all he could not to cry.
"That's not much of a hope, is it?"
He did a double take as if there were something about me he hadn't noticed before. "That's what any of you would say," he said.

When you're talking to someone with absolute belief—and in this case there was no half-amused, sly smile to undermine his conviction—it shakes your own sense of reality, which is what I said to Helena.
"Joel's always been full of shit," she said. "You take him too seriously. You guys always have."
And that's when I got in trouble with Helena, not so much for defending Joel as for defending the way I wanted to perceive him. And while we argued, bad feelings turning to worse, I had the bizarre sense that this was not the Helena I had been living with in affectionate companionship for fourteen years—our fifteenth anniversary was just three months away—but a barely convincing imposter.

3

Events move too quickly here to track them with the kind of cause-and-effect detail that particularizes them for the reader. About two months (perhaps three) after our "talk" at the Brass Bar, Joel was institutionalized for depression. My source for this information was Helena, who was in daily telephone contact with Dotty and whose conversations I sometimes eavesdropped on from my study with the door ajar, missing the equivalent of every third word. So I knew Dotty's representation of events, or as much of it as Helena was willing to share, but almost nothing of Joel's side. I did reach him once on the phone after several failed tries (the story was he went two weeks without a word to anyone), and was subjected to a brief rant before he hung up or the phone was taken from him. A few lines from what I think of now as a cry for help have stayed with me.

"They know I'm onto them," he said. "One of these days, you can set your watch on it, they're going to put me out of commission. They're going to…. I can't say any more. Shhh. Someone's coming. When it happens, you'll know." Other times when I tried to reach him, I was told he didn't want to come to the phone. Once by Dotty, once by the older daughter, who was staying over after the breakup of her marriage.

Joel's ostensible depression has created an ever-widening invisible rift between Helena and me. I say invisible because in public, for the most part, we are our old selves together. In private, uncharacteristically, she shows almost no compassion for Joel's condition. One day, after one of her extended conversations with Dotty, she told me, "She's finally beginning to be able to admit to herself that she's happier without him."

"Is that a positive?"

"Why wouldn't it be? I don't understand what you're asking. We want Dotty to feel better about her life, don't we?"

"What about Joel?"

"This has nothing to do with Joel. Joel is of no use to Dotty in his present state. Joel is lost, and maybe always has been. He doesn't live in the same world as the rest of us."

This is where our conversation would break off and I would think, wanting to see Helena in the best possible light, that maybe she doesn't mean these remarks as harshly as they sound to me.

And then one afternoon, when Helena is out of town visiting her parents, I go to see a revival of Tarkovsky's *Solaris* and make a discovery that has nothing to do with the film. Almost directly in front of me—perhaps three rows separate us—I note the back of a head that looks very much like Dotty's. When the film ends, I wait patiently for her to exit the row. What I haven't noticed is that there is a man with her, someone I think I know but can't place, and they are whispering to each other as they pass. I have to call her name to get her attention, and even then it takes an extra moment for her to turn around. She greets me warmly—I've actually known Dotty longer than I've known Joel—and without hesitation (or perhaps the slightest hesitation) she introduces me to her companion as if there were nothing unacceptable in my finding them together. Her self-possession is almost too good to be true. We stop briefly at a local coffee shop and when discussion of the movie is out of the way, I ask how Joel is doing. "It's hard to say," she says. "They say he's making progress, but when I see him I'm not always sure what they mean by progress."

"I never knew that Joel had problems with depression," I say.

"It's very recent with him," she says. "He's had bouts of depression before, but nothing remotely like what he's been going through."

While we talk, her companion, whose name eludes me, observes our conversation like an eavesdropper, watchful and silent.

For some reason I can't explain, I neglect to mention this chance meeting with Dotty to Helena, who, for all I know, knows more about the friendship with this other man than I do.

Though I don't remember exactly how it started, or even when, each morning before I go to work on my novel, I study the front page of the *New York Times* and find stories that conform with only the smallest of stretch to Joel's shapeshifter alien theory. I discuss this with no one, not Helena, not even my therapist, though I have acquired a notebook in which I jot down these instances for future reference. I have the idea, which I realize is naïve and even a little dimwitted, of taking the notebook with me when I get around to visiting Joel (he's been at the Forestvale Depression Center for almost eight months now) in the hope of cheering him up. It should cheer him to know that there are outside sources that confirm his most unacceptable beliefs.

I can't say why I waited so long before visiting Joel at Forestvale, which is, in any event, a time-consuming thirty-two-mile drive from the city. I have been thinking of going for a while, but I always find some excuse at the last moment to avoid the trip. One morning, however, this morning in fact, I decide to go without subjecting the impulse to rational consideration. I have already driven a few blocks when I realize I have forgotten the notebook I have been assembling for Joel, and I drive back to retrieve it, the notion of postponing the trip once again making a brief, uninvited visit of its own.

The main building, though formidably grim on approach, is a lot more cheerful on the inside than I might have imagined. The walls are decorated with travel posters for exotic places.

A perky white-haired woman who seems to be in charge warns me as we make our way to Joel's room that he might not recognize me at first. Patients who go through the shock treatment sequence, she says, tend to lose some immediate memory. It turns out that Joel is not in his quarters, and Mrs. Gassner, my guide, taken aback by his unexpected absence, actually looks under the bed before taking me to the common room. "He usually keeps to his own space," she says. "That he's out is a positive sign. I usually have to get one of the aides to take him to lunch."

We find a crumpled version of Joel sitting by himself in front of a TV set that has not been turned on. "Joel, you have a visitor," she says to him in her chirpy voice. Then to me: "You're his brother, I assume. The resemblance is striking."

"No," I say.

Finally, Joel turns to look at us, and there is a benign smile on his face I can't remember having seen before.

"Joel, your brother is here to see you," she says.

"Thank you for coming," he says stiffly, getting up from his chair, narrowing his eyes to assess me.

Eventually, Mrs. Gassner leaves us to ourselves, though not before finding us a place to talk—we're set up at opposites sides of a card table—away from the other patients. I have difficulty knowing where to start.

"Are they treating you well?" I ask.

"What do you think?" he says. "No really, I'm fine. Couldn't be better. Who sent you?"

"You don't recognize me, do you? I'm Josh."

"Of course I recognize you," he says. "You're Josh, aren't you? What do you want, Josh?"

The longer we talk, the less it seems to me that the man sitting across from me is Joel. Or to put it another way, his Joelness, the qualities I think of that define Joel, have been diminished to virtual absence.

And then maybe forty minutes into our conversation, averting his eyes which have momentarily come into focus, he says, "You don't need to believe everything she says about me."

"I don't," I say. "Everything who says?"

"You know who," he says. "I can tell by looking at you that you know. She's got to justify herself. We all need to maintain our own realities in the face of the evidence amassed against us."

I don't disagree.

It is at this point I think of showing Joel the notebook with its corroborating evidence, but then I realize that I've forgotten to take it from the car. When I try to tell him about it—it is not easy to explain without an immediate context—Joel claps his hands over his ears. "I don't know where you got that," he says.

"I didn't mean to upset you."

Eventually, he removes his hands from his ears and offers me another version of his eerie benign smile. "Don't get your tits in an uproar," he says. "Forget it, okay? If you're not in the water yourself, Josh, it's imprudent to make waves.... The thing to remember, Josh, the single most important thing, Josh, is that there are no crazy people in madhouses."

When I get up to leave, we don't shake hands, but Joel thanks me again for my visit before turning abruptly away.

4

Barely a month after Joel comes home from Forestvale, Dotty gives a party to which most or all of Joel's closest friends are invited. On the way over, Helena and I have the following conversation in the car.

"Is she unhappier now that he's returned?" I ask her.

"I know you're kidding," she says, "and I don't know the answer to your question, but it's possible. More than possible. When you get used to living alone, it's hard to have someone invading your space again. You know as well as I do that Joel has never been easy to live with."

If I knew that, I can't remember knowing it, which is what I say though not quite in those words. "Then it's especially nice of her to make this party for him."

"Oh, Dotty's a good person," she says. "Though if you don't want to be alone with someone, it's protective to have other people around."

"And you think that's the reason for this party, to have other people around?"

"No, though it's possible. I have no specific information one way or another."

There are nine other guests when we arrive, but, oddly in my opinion, no sign of Joel, who, according to Dotty, has gone out to pick up some more beer.

Helena rolls her eyes at the news, but Dotty gives no indication that anything's amiss. "More people are coming, it turns out, than we originally expected. Joel thought it would be a bad omen to run out of beer at his own welcome home party." There is an understated WELCOME HOME, JOEL sign taped to the refrigerator door.

I tend to drink moderately these days—two glasses of wine at most in an evening—but tonight for some reason, perhaps some anxiety on Joel's behalf, I go past my usual limit. After my third or fourth glass—all put away before Joel's return—I see no point in keeping further count.

"Please don't get drunk on me," Helena says to me in passing, but by that time I'm too far along to care.

I am aware that I've said some outrageous things to people, some of whom I barely know; the looks I've gotten in exchange are my evidence. I see what I'm doing, when I think about it at all—I try to remain as oblivious as possible—as a kind of allegiance to Joel.

I am not aware of the exact moment of Joel's return, only that at some point he is there at the center of a crowd, talking to a woman who earlier in the evening—I have only the vaguest sense of when— told me to "fuck off." And what could I possibly have said to her to have provoked such unpleasantness? In waiting for Joel to extricate himself, I lose sight of him again.

I haven't had my opportunity to wish Joel well when Helena comes by with my coat over her arm. "I think it's about time I got you home," she says.

"I haven't talked to my friend Joel yet," I say.

"Oh dear," she says. "You seem to have insulted everyone else. Okay, sweetheart. Go say goodbye to Joel, and I'll say goodbye to Dotty, who I suspect won't be the least bit unhappy to see us go. Josh, promise me, okay?—that you'll talk to no one else but Joel."

I can't make that promise, I tell her, though in the spirit of compromise I put down the mostly finished glass of wine in my hand on the first surface that approaches before going to look for my friend.

It takes the opening and closing of several doors—there is a couple necking in one of the guest bedrooms, and for a moment I think the man is Joel—before I find him sitting by himself in the dark in the TV room, which also serves as a library.

"How's it hanging, buddy?" I greet him. "Helena says it's time for us to go."

"Who is it?" he asks.

"It's me," I say, "though the correct answer is it is I."

"It's good of you to come, me," he says. "I'm all of a sudden extremely tired of talking to people. Can you imagine? I'm not used to staying up this late anymore. Goodnight, me."

"Goodnight, buddy," I say. "It's been a great party, except for the handful of extraterrestrials that slipped in under false pretenses."

"Ah hah," he says. "If I were you, me, I'd let my wife do the driving home."

As if on cue, Helena comes up on me from behind and takes me by the arm, leading me out of the house with only verbal resistance on my part. I seem to sleep most of the ride home, though there is an unfriendly one-sided conversation going on between us in the interstices.

When I go to bed that night, pressed up against Helena's back in our king-sized bed, the earliest stages of self-righteous anger and regret beginning to overtake me, I wonder what Joel was thinking during our abbreviated conversation. I think he didn't know me in the dark or want to know me, whoever I was. He'll figure it out, I suspect, or not. Helena will find a way to forgive me in the morning. Or not. I meant well, I hear myself think as consciousness like bathwater seeps down the drain. I have the sense of watching myself fall asleep.

I dream of hiding out in an anonymous room at the far end of a house I lived in as a child, someone trying to get in, whoever ratcheting the handle at the side door. I refuse to panic, rehearse in my head the details of a hopelessly elaborate means of escape, while awaiting the inevitable arrival of the body snatcher who has my name printed in black magic marker clipped to the pocket of his shirt.

OFFICE HOURS

I usually keep my door locked during office hours, not wanting to give the random eager student the wrong impression. I'm opposed to conferences, though I make myself available as required—I hang out at my desk one hour a week for just that purpose—but I see no point in unfelt encouragement. You have to knock at least three times to get me to open the door. So only the persistent, who usually visit with an agenda of complaint, get in to see me, and it is the persistent who are generally the most tiresome. So much of college teaching, so much of life, is wasting time in the disguise of conversation. Whatever small wisdom I have to impart has already been imparted in lectures or in the margins of papers I've graded. So, as the more perceptive of my students note, the way to gain my respect is to stay away.

The above is all prelude, of course, to my describing an experience in 180-degree opposition to my hard-earned expectations. And it happens with someone—a woman, a graduate student—who had come in on the wrong day to see the person who uses my office on the days I'm not there. This is what she said to me when, against better judgment, I opened the door to let her in on her fifth barely audible knock. She looked at me with narrowed eyes and said accusingly, "You're not Professor Haggert."

"Haggert is in on Mondays and Wednesdays," I said.

Nevertheless she walked by me and sat down in the chair next to my desk. "What day is today?" she asked, as if she had caught me in some kind of self-contradiction.

My first impression was that she had been crying or had spent a sleepless night or both. She wasn't a bad-looking woman, though she was clearly not at her best, whatever that might have been.

"Today was Tuesday when I woke up this morning," I said.

"Are you positive?" she said. "When I woke up it was Wednesday."

So here was this woman I'd never met—I did have the sense that I'd seen her before somewhere or other but still—storming into my office to argue about what day it was. "If it was Wednesday," I said, "Haggert would have been here instead of me."

"And we both would have been happier," she said. "Or maybe not."

"Something like that," I said.

"Would you give Professor Haggert a message?"

"The thing is, Ms....I never see Haggert. We're not here on the same days. You could leave him a note."

"No," she said. "I could but I can't. A note has too much permanence."

I laughed, assuming she had made a joke, but in the next moment I realized that had not been her intent. She was tearing up, foraging in her purse for something with which to wipe her eyes or blow her nose. Nothing emerged and she used the back of her hand to blot her eyes.

"Are you all right?" I said, not knowing what else to say, embarrassed at the poverty of my sympathy.

"Yes...no," she said. "Would it be all right if I told you something? Sometimes it's easier to talk to someone you don't know. You have a sympathetic presence."

That was not my reputation, and as a probable consequence her remark flattered me into letting her continue. "In that case..." I said.

"I've gotten myself into something that feels inescapable," she said. "What I'm saying is, I don't know how to bring it to an end."

"Is this an academic matter?"

"Well, it is and it isn't. Some might consider it a personal matter, but that's not the way it started. If it's something that took place at the college, it's an academic matter, isn't it? By definition."

"I see," the persona of my sympathetic presence said.

"I'm older than most graduate students, not that much older but older, and at least then I was otherwise unattached. That's the only reason I took him up on his offer."

"His offer?"

"We had been having a conference dealing with this piece I had written and he suggested that we continue it, the conference, over dinner. That's pretty much how it started. It was the natural continuation of a discussion we had been having. And what happened afterward was predictable if I had taken the time to think about, you know, the implicit context."

"Okay," I said. "Is this Professor Haggert we're talking about?"

"Is it all right with you if I don't mention any names? I'm not looking to hurt anyone's reputation."

"That's a good thing," I said, "though you never know—it might enhance whoever's reputation."

She looked at me uncertainly, then shook her head and permitted herself a very small smile. "That was meant as a joke, right? People tell me I have zero sense of humor. You'll have to get used to that."

"Will I?"

She laughed. "I didn't mean that the way you seem to think I meant it."

That's when someone else knocked at the door and my visitor got out of her seat in a kind of mock slow motion. "I'll come back another time," she said. "I don't want to interfere with your job."

When she finally made her way out, whoever was on the other side of the door was also gone.

I had no expectations of seeing her again, but when she didn't show up the same time or any time after that the following Tuesday, it unmade my day.

The week after that, I left my office door unlocked during my posted office hour but no one I wanted to see showed up. One of the department secretaries stuck her head in to tell me that I hadn't turned in last term's grade book. The reason for that, which I explained to her for about the third time, is that I don't use grade books.

When three weeks went by without a return visit, my accidental visitor began to grow in beauty and whatever virtues attended beauty. On the other hand, I wondered if I crossed her path in another context, say somewhere off campus, would I even recognize her. Her image remained strong if variable in memory. I cursed myself for not having remembered her name, though perhaps it had never been offered.

I came into the college the following Monday on an unacknowledged fact-finding tour disguised as an unavoidable errand. Haggert was in my office when I came in, conferencing with a student who was not remotely the one I was half hoping to find, planning to ask Haggert about my visitor and possibly uncover the level of involvement between them. For no apparent reason, Haggert and I had a kind of low-level antipathy going on between us. My irritation growing by the minute, I sat impatiently in the anteroom until chronic bad disposition got the better of me. Looking to pass the time with less duress, I went down to the student cafeteria for a cup of coffee.

The Java Jive concession was open, which was not always the case, and I treated myself to a "giant" cappuccino, which was in fact the smallest size they served.

I didn't want arbitrary company, so I made my way toward an empty table I had spotted at the far end of the cafeteria. A disembodied voice interrupted my journey.

"There's an unoccupied chair here," it (she) said.

"That's all right," I said, before registering the source of the voice, a familiar-looking woman I couldn't quite place.

No need to be coy. It was the woman who had visited my office and I hadn't, not wholly, not at the moment, recognized her.

"If you'd rather sit by yourself," she said, her smile taunting me, "I'd understand."

"You look different today," I said, taking the seat across from her as opposed to the one alongside.

"My hair may have been up the other day," she said. "Was that it? You also look somewhat different, you know. Did you get a haircut or something?"

"No. You seem less upset today," I said. "I suppose you've extricated yourself from the troubling relationship you mentioned."

"Well, no," she said. "And I'd appreciate it if you lowered your voice. I didn't mean that the way it announced itself. If I looked happier, it's because I'm happy to see you again."

I didn't know what to make of her remark. "Thank you, I guess," I said.

"You guess? What does that mean?"

"You know you never told me your name."

"Are you sure? I thought I did. Anyway, you could have asked your colleague about me. And maybe you have."

"If I had—when you say colleague, you mean Haggert, don't you?—then I'd know your name."

"My friends call me Helena, Professor. Maybe that's because Helena's my name."

"Helena," I said.

"I have to go to class now. It was nice running into you."

I thought of inviting her to come by the office tomorrow to continue our talk, but I let the thought pass for the deed. "I enjoyed our conversation," I said.

"That's nice, Professor," she said. "I was actually thinking about you the very moment you hurried by my table, pretending not to notice me. So you might say I conjured your presence." And then she held out her hand to me to shake, the gesture mocking itself.

I wanted to watch her leave, a way of holding on, but I let her vanish with hardly a glance in her direction.

When I returned to my shared office, Haggert's door was closed. He was speaking to a female student and I could make out voices, though very little that was actually said. On the way home it struck me that the woman's voice that had leached back to me through the space under the door was Helena's. It annoyed me that she hadn't mentioned that she was leaving me to see Haggert.

I might as well say it now. I have a history of obsessive behavior, which I try, almost always unsuccessfully, to resist. In light of that, I thought it best not to see Helena again, particularly so because I was wasting much too much interior time obsessing about this disturbingly undefined relationship.

So during my next office hour, I made a point of locking my door, prepared to ignore the imprecations of anyone hoping to see me. All in vain. There were no tempting knocks to resist. As a matter of fact, there were no untempting ones either. Nevertheless, I found it impossible to read the student work in front of me, my heightened attention focused on the door for the entire seemingly endless hour.

It was that no one came by to test my resolve that ultimately defeated that resolve, or so I interpret the fact that, the following Tuesday, she was once again in the hard-backed chair catty-corner to my desk. I had unthinkingly left the door open; she had slouched in without bothering to knock, catching me in an odd mood.

She seemed forlorn once again, breakable. My ungrateful stare said what are you doing here and so she defended herself. "You said," she began, "that if I needed to talk I could come back."

"I didn't expect to see you again," I said.

"Does that mean you want me to leave? You let me think your door was always open to me."

"You're here," I said. "Tell me what you want to tell me."

"It was a mistake to come here, wasn't it? I didn't know where else to go. That's not precisely true. I came here because I wanted to see you."

"It wasn't a mistake to come," I said.

"I'm presuming on your goodwill," she said. "You must think I'm terrible. Do you? It's confusing to me that you share the same office."

"I can imagine," I said. "Are you still seeing the faculty member—you see, I mention no names—that took you to dinner?"

She considered the question at some length before saying, "I don't know. We've taken turns breaking off with the other, but it doesn't stick. We have difficulty, or at least it seems that way, keeping apart. Having to see him in tutorial doesn't make it any easier."

"You could drop the tutorial."

"I can't," she said. "I need the class for my degree. Besides, the term is barely half over."

"It's not can't," I said. "It's won't. You could stop coming to tutorial and get your degree. He wouldn't have the nerve to stand in your way. You don't want to stop seeing him or you would."

She turned her face away. "Sometimes I do," she said.

"What times are those?"

"I can't answer that," she said. "I guess when I'm feeling better about myself. When I'm with you, I think I can stop. He's married, you know, but they don't get along."

"No one has ever told his mistress that he gets along with his wife," I said. "I don't know of anyone who has."

"You don't like him one bit, do you?" she said with a surprising show of anger.

"What I'm telling you has nothing to do with my feelings for the unmentionable. Besides, I hardly know him."

"He's a colleague, isn't he? You share an office with him. How can you be so mean about him?"

"We're in on different days. I never attend department meetings. But that's beside the point. I'm responding to what you tell me. He's an invisible factor in this for me."

She gave me a skeptical look, got herself up, and left the office.

I regretted having left my door open. For one reason or another, I always regret being available.

The following Tuesday, I pretended to myself that her repeated knocks, her shy persistence, were someone else's, and I got up from my desk to open the door for her.

She sat down in her usual seat and stared at her hands while we both waited for one of us to speak. "If you're expecting an apology," she said at last, "you're not going to get it." Then she broke up laughing.

I didn't let on how pleased I was to see her. "What's new?" I said.

"You're going to be proud of me," she said. "I didn't go to tutorial yesterday. He actually called me at home last night to ask me why."

"What did you tell him?"

"I was so overjoyed he called, I couldn't tell him the real reason. I said something about not feeling up to coming. It was a half truth. What should I have said?"

"I'm the wrong person to ask."

"No. What would you have said if you were in my shoes?"

I shook my head. "Does he know about us, about your visits to me?"

"No," she said. "He might. I think I might have mentioned about coming in the wrong day that time and discovering someone else in his place."

There had been an unsigned note clipped to my desk calendar when I came in today, which read in its entirety, STAY OUT OF MY BUSINESS PLEASE! "What did you say about me?"

"I don't know. I said how kind you were and he said that's not your reputation in the department. He said you have the reputation of being a curmudgeon. Is that true?"

"How do I know," I said, "though it could also be that your friend, for his own good reasons, is universalizing a private perception."

"He said you keep your door locked in order to avoid your students. You do keep your door locked during office hours, don't you?"

"I let you in," I said.

The following week, my door unlocked, Haggert appeared in our shared office on the wrong day.

"Do you have an appointment?" I asked, not looking up from the book I was reading.

"I think you know why I'm here," he said.

"That's presumptuous of you," I said. "Is there something I can do to help you?"

He remained standing, which made him look larger than he actually was. "Everyone knows what a prick you are," he said. "I was hoping that we could have a civilized talk."

"Have a seat," I said.

He hesitated, considered other unapparent options, before oc-cupying the seat next to the desk. "You're making this hard for me," he said.

"If I have," I said, "it may be the only thing right I've done so far. What do you want? Does this have something to do with Helena?"

"There are people around, mutual acquaintances, who say that you are actually not as big a prick as you seem. I tend to look for the best in others."

"I get that you don't like me," I said. "Your point has been made. I take it as an inadvertent compliment that you don't like me. That said, I don't see any point in continuing this discussion, do you?"

"Look, I'm sorry if I offended you," he said. "I'm in an edgy mood. My purpose in coming here is to speak to your better nature."

"My better nature?" I withheld a laugh.

"Does that amuse you?" he said. "Ms. Golden, Helena, is much more fragile than she may appear. I'm asking you out of common decency to stay away from her."

"That's an odd request, coming from you."

"As her teacher and her friend, I'm asking you to keep away from her. You think you can manage that?"

"It sounds to me as if you're talking to yourself," I said. "And who are you, you sanctimonious asshole, to throw the word decency at anyone? As I understand it, though it's not a word I would ordinar-ily use, you're the one who's behaved indecently."

It was at that moment that a comic strip light bulb seemed to go on over his head. "Wait a minute. You think Helena and I…. Where did you get that idea? No. No. I'm not the one taking advantage of her. She let me believe…you are involved with her, aren't you?"

"No such luck," I said.

———

After the meeting with Haggert, I was near terminally disappointed with Helena, though I also half hoped that she would show up in my office again, which didn't happen for a while. I wanted to believe, had a stake in believing, that Helena was not quite the manipulative liar that Haggert's revelations suggested. It all made sense in a certain way. And none of it did. What reason did Helena have to lie to me? And why did she lie to Haggert about me? At the very least, I was curious to hear her side of things.

I accessed her phone number and thought of calling her at home, but characteristically I didn't. It was my MO, a former therapist once told me, to avoid messy entanglements.

What I did instead was call one of her former teachers, a woman who had visited in the writing program last year, a sometime friend, with whom (I feel obliged to report) I had had a very brief affair more than three years ago.

We met at a restaurant/bar almost equidistant between our two Brooklyn apartments, a place we had been to before when it was under different ownership.

I got to the point before the small talk, the what-had-we-each-been-up-to talk, was fully concluded. "Jane, how did Helena Golden do in your workshop?" I asked.

"I like her writing," she said. "I just wish she had done more of it. She wrote three stories for me, very short stories, none of which had an ending. She's got ability."

"Yes. What did you think of her as a person?"

"Before I answer that, Jake, I want to know why you're asking. What's going on? Are you doing something you shouldn't be doing? Of course it's none of my business."

I considered telling Jane the entire story, but after a brief in-head debate, I decided not to. Perhaps I was protecting Helena, though at the moment I thought I was protecting myself. Even from the vantage of my perception of it, the story I had to tell didn't quite parse. "It's not even my business," I said.

"We became friends for a while," Jane said, pausing, taking two extended sips from her wine glass, "and then we stopped being friends. You still haven't told me why you're asking about her."

"Did you stop being friends with her because you discovered she didn't always tell the truth?"

"No. Not exactly. Who always tells the truth? This is making me uncomfortable, Jake. I'm not going to say anything else about Helena unless you tell me specifically why you want to know."

"I'd rather not," I said. "You'll have to trust my reasons."

"Do you mind if I order some food?" she asked, summoning our waitress. "I haven't eaten anything since breakfast."

"Of course not," I said, but once I realized that I was not likely to learn any more about Helena from her, I was eager to get away. "I have to be somewhere in an hour," I said.

"Really?"

The edgy dynamic of our former intimacy seemed to be reasserting itself. "There's plenty of time for you to eat," I said. I ordered a third glass of wine and a slice of chocolate pudding cake to help pass the time. When Jane finished her salad, which she seemed to be eating in slow motion, I drove her home. After we said goodnight with a peremptory hug and I accepted with some reluctance her invitation to come in for a nightcap, she confided that she felt protective of Helena because they had once, actually twice, slept together.

As I said, Helena didn't visit my office again for quite some time, and when I thought about it, I told myself that it was on balance for the best. Throughout this period, my door was open to anyone who wanted to come and talk to me. Occasionally, someone or other actually did.

The day of my last class, I found an unsigned note in my mailbox, saying, whoever it might be, that the writer would like to talk to me at my convenience. It offered, its only specific information, a Manhattan phone number.

I waited an hour and twenty-seven minutes before calling and got a recorded message announcing that no one was available to answer. I left no message in return.

Shortly after going to sleep that night—it was probably not quite as late as it seemed—my phone rang. In the middle of a dream, I stumbled out of the coffin of sleep to answer it. "Someone called me from your number," a woman's voice said.

"It must have been me," I said. "Do you think you can come by my office tomorrow at about one?"

"I don't know," she said. "I'll try."

I arrived at my office at ten after one the next day, anticipating my caller waiting at the door for my arrival. No one was there, which was equally predictable, and I regretted with renewed bitterness having made the trip. I picked up my mail and returned to my office to see if there was anything that required attention. Someone had left me a copy of the college literary magazine, *Whispers*, which was the only thing in the pile that had even the slightest entertainment value. I took turns browsing and dozing.

A series of knocks at the door interrupted my reading of a story called "Hasty Retreats" by Helena Golden. The narrative had some familiar elements. The plot concerned a woman who had taken up the writing of fiction after a few other failed careers. Unsure of what she was doing, she presented what were imagined situations to her teachers as if they were actual events in her life.

Though the knocking persisted, I wanted to see how her story played out before whoever it was invaded my space, so I skip-read my way to the end.

In the last paragraph of the story, the forty-year-old female graduate student slowly opens the door to her professor's office after he has ignored her repeated knocking. "Look, I'm sorry," she calls to him on entering. "Will you, can you, forgive me?"

"Never," he calls back without hesitation.

The story concludes: "But her professor has gotten out of his chair and is half-facing toward her. It pleases her to see from his body language, which she has studied in the imagination's text as if she might be tested on it, that, whatever his other virtues, he is not to be believed when matters of the heart are at stake."

LOST CAR

It starts with my coming out of a movie, sometimes with someone—my wife, one of my former wives—and not remembering where exactly I parked the car. I don't panic, I never panic. What I do is try to visualize the various streets I traversed to get to the theater, some memorable landmarks which might help determine the way there and consequently the way back. As I tend to be destination oriented, this method of inquiry inevitably yields a faceless landscape. More potent is the memory of driving around looking for a place to park against the self-induced pressure of arriving at the movie on time. I can see the car now in my mind's eye parked behind an exceptionally wide van or SUV, black or dark green, the space unlit.

And then, walking toward my idea of where the car is, I think I see it in the distance, not behind a van of uncertain color (that might have been another time altogether) but behind a car very much like it, which may indeed even be the car itself. Closer inspection yields disappointment. My "metallic mist" Honda Civic (perhaps Corolla) has Massachusetts plates last I looked, and both the cars I have focused on as potentially mine have New York plates. So much for expectation. The street I parked on is similar, indeed almost identical to the one I am on, but it is, so evidence or lack thereof suggests, a different street in the same general area. I can remember now finding no spaces on this street and turning right and then right again and finding a secreted space between two huge SUVs on this other parallel street. I hurry over to this other street while the sense memory of my parking there remains fresh. The second street is darker than the first. It is always that way.

By this time, I have chased after my parked car on four different streets, each with its own persuasive claim in fickle memory and, need I even say it, without success. In the past, when I've been unable to find my car after giving more than sufficient time to the search, I saw no point in beating myself up over it. So I conceded the loss and got home by other means. Perhaps the car had been stolen—what other explanation could there be, I had pretty much covered the area looking for it—and so, as I depended on a car, I considered buying a new one, or perhaps a previously owned one in near-new condition, though a native caution restrained me from rushing into something I might later regret. At the same time, I saw no point in sacrificing my life to a seemingly endless search for an unrecoverable object, no matter my affection for it. I've been in this situation, I admit with some reluctance, more than once, and I have avoided excessive despair in each case. Sanity, as I see it, is knowing when to throw away false hope. In my weaker moments, I concede that the world is haunted.

The above was what Joshua told Clarissa, his dinner companion, a woman he had met through a matchmaking service on the Internet in which applicants filled out a detailed personality profile. Clarissa had asked him for a revealing anecdote about himself and he took the risk of telling her about his disappeared car. They had made a point of sharing embarrassing stories as a way of getting to know the other while easing the awkwardness of what was, after all, a blind date. His counselor from the MatchesMadeInHeaven.com service had told him unofficially that Clarissa's personality profile indicated an unusual capacity for empathy, and so Josh was cautiously hopeful of being understood without being judged.

A woman with an interestingly ruined face, Clarissa was, in her own words, a former litigations lawyer who, having risen from the ashes of a midlife crisis, had reinvented herself as a psychotherapist. Josh, on the other hand, had attended medical school without completing the course, had published two books of poems and a mystery novel (under a pseudonym), had taught, at different times in his life, history, Renaissance poetry, and filmmaking, and was currently the book review editor of a small, highly respected journal of opinion with extremely limited financial resources. Since his divorce six months ago, he tended to eat most of his meals out, though at less upscale places than the one Clarissa had chosen for their first date.

He couldn't exactly say why, but there was something about Clarissa that spoke to his deepest urges. Moments after she sat down across from him, he fantasized undressing her in slow motion, pressing his face into her slightly protruding belly, sliding his tongue down the incline into the sweet space between her legs. It was not a usual urge, and he wondered if this was what it was like to connect with one's soulmate.

"I don't think we're all that much alike," she said to him at one point, "and I mean that, I really do, as a positive."

Her assertion soured his mood. "How so?"

"Well," she said, "for one, if I misplaced something that I valued, I wouldn't give up looking for it until I recovered it."

"I used to be that way," he said, "but I've learned to be less absolute."

"I wasn't being critical of you," she said. "Did you think I was?"

This was when the waiter appeared to take their orders and Josh discovered that Clarissa had ordered the very entree he had in mind for himself, which put him in a temporary bind. To assert that he was his own person, he ordered instead something he had no intention of ordering, something he had always wanted to try but had managed up until now to avoid, a spur-of-the-moment improvisatory maneuver.

"I don't know what to make of your choice," she said. "I was told that your profile indicated we have similar tastes in food and that, like me, what you put in your mouth is important to you. Herman and I—Herman was my second husband—always used to order the same entrees in restaurants; that is, until I discovered I was accommodating myself to his tastes, which were not mine at all."

Often without warning—it was an aspect of the haunted thing—attraction would turn into repulsion for him and back again like changes in the weather. "Look," he said, "I need to get this off my chest so there'll be no misunderstanding down the road. I'm not really looking for a long-term relationship." Listening to himself, he deplored his crudeness, but at the same time he was pleased, as it seemed to him, to clear the air.

"Good," she said. "It's a relief to have that out of the way." She held out her hand for him to shake, which he took with gratitude after a moment's hesitation followed by internal crosswinds of wonder and trepidation. Whatever he had agreed to, it was an agreement whose terms remained elusive.

When the waiter delivered dessert menus, Clarissa turned them away with a wave of her hand. "We can do better than this at my place," she said. "I have two-thirds of a very good pear cobbler and some excellent French roast decaf. How does that sound?"

"Isn't it getting late?" he said, looking at his watch for confirmation after the question.

She gave him a sympathetic smile punctuated by a charming, perhaps even seductive shrug. "It's not late for me," she said. "I'm a night person."

A huge raucous laugh went up at the table behind them, a chorus of near-hysterical discordant amusement. At first it seemed to be a table of eight women, but then he noticed that one of them, the one apparently amusing the others, was a man with a ponytail.

When the check arrived, Clarissa covered it with her hand and edged it over to her side of the table. "This is mine," she said.

"Why don't we just split it," he said, but by the time he extracted his credit card from his wallet, she had already handed the bill, trumped with her own plastic, to a passing waiter. He felt defeated and somewhat embittered. "I'll get the next one," he said.

"I'll hold you to it," she said.

More shrill laughter from the table behind them, one of the women falling out of her chair with a thump and an ear-shattering squeal, to applause from the others.

On the way out of the restaurant, the oldest-looking of the women at the noisy table winked at him as he passed.

The advertised pear cobbler had a suspicion of mold at the edges and Clarissa, sighing her apology, scraped both plates into the garbage with an unnerving decisiveness.

"It's all right," Josh said, more disturbed by Clarissa's abruptness than the loss of dessert. It felt to him somehow as if he had been the one discarded.

"Why don't we go to bed for dessert," she said, "and after that, if something else is required, I'll make us a pot of coffee."

"Clarissa, if it's all right with you, I'd prefer having my coffee before dessert," he said, postponing what he wanted (or didn't) most.

"Oh my God," she said. "I totally knew you were going to say that, I could have spoken your lines for you."

"Really?" he said. "And what am I going to say now?"

"You were going to ask the very question you just asked," she said, laughing.

He considered his options as if he had several, wanting to reclaim his uniqueness by doing something she would never have anticipated.

So striving for the unexpected, he opted for sex before coffee and afterward rejected the coffee option and went home before she was ready to part with him.

The next morning he thought of phoning Clarissa, but kept finding reasons to postpone what hardwired instinct told him was a necessary gesture.

And so when the phone rang late in the afternoon, he had no doubts who was on the line. "Have you been thinking of calling me?" were her first words.

He would never again, he told himself, get involved with a woman with a similar personality profile. "As usual, you're on to me," he said.

"And so why didn't you?"

"Why didn't I what?"

"Why didn't you call when you were thinking about it?"

He assumed it was a rhetorical question since, as the evidence suggested, she knew him better than he knew himself. After worrying the question, he made the only answer their dialogue allowed. "I didn't call," he said, "so as not to deny you the opportunity to call first and ask if I'd been thinking of calling you."

His remark, which he meant to be charming, produced a jagged hole in the conversation. "If you say so," she said after the silence had extended itself into the anxiety of unknown territory.

He was about to say he was glad that he hadn't lost her when she said, "Pigeon shit," and hung up. She was gone before he could register his surprise at what seemed a wholly uncharacteristic response.

A former wife, a former former wife, used to hang up on him when he said something she didn't want to hear (or anticipated not wanting to hear what he hadn't yet said), and the recollection doubled his anger at Clarissa. If he called back, which was his first impulse (already replaced), he would tell her how much he hated to be hung up on. In the end, he decided against calling her until, if ever, he was in a position to forgive her dismissal of him.

He imagined Clarissa thinking she never wanted to hear from him again and he was strangely comforted by the realization that, on such short acquaintance, they had already achieved a near-unbreachable rift in their undefined relationship.

The next day he called MatchesMadeInHeaven.com and told his counselor that he didn't think it was going to work out with Clarissa. What other matches were there with his name on them? "I'll re-evaluate your profile," the counselor said, "and get back to you."

Clarissa called later in the week to tell him of a dream she had concerning him. "In this dream," she said, "we were leaving a movie together—it was a Japanese horror film, in which characters transformed according to certain inner qualities—and I suddenly knew—it couldn't have been more lucid—I knew without a doubt where your lost car was, and I led you to it. The odd thing was that you were displeased at my finding it for you and I was sorry—this was also very clear in the dream—I was sorry that I had gone out of my way to help you."

"I see," he said, not seeing at all.

"You don't see," she said. "Josh, the dream was extremely vivid, and if you'll take me on as your guide, so to speak, I have the feeling that I can find your lost car for you. There's one provision you'll have to agree to first."

"Okay," he said, "what do I have to agree to?"

"You have to promise in advance that you'll be pleased to get it back. Can you promise that?"

"Why did you hang up on me last time we talked?" he asked.

There were a few beats of silence before she spoke and he wondered if he had inadvertently invited being cut off again.

"When did I hang up on you?" she asked, her tone aggrieved. "Why would I hang up on you?"

"Well," he said, "you hung up on me because apparently you were offended at something I said," he said.

"Offended, huh?" she said. "If you knew why I hung up on you, why did you ask me the reason?"

"I'm willing to let the subject drop," he said, "whatever the subject."

When they arrived at the movie theater to begin their search, Clarissa corroborated that his local nine-plex, grandiosely called the Pavilion, was indeed much like the theater in her dream.

They walked slowly, hand in hand, checking out each car they passed, and he felt, not for the first time, that there was something uncanny between them. Nevertheless, he found himself hoping that the unlikely, the near impossible, was not going to triumph over what he liked to think of as common sense.

She pulled him to a stop at a nondescript Honda with Massachusetts plates and he hesitated, not quite looking at the car, before denying that it was his.

"Are you sure?" she asked.

The question outraged him. "Don't you think I know my own car?"

"You have to admit," she said, "the coincidence is impressive, wouldn't you say?"

"Yes…no…who knows," he said. "Despite the impressive coincidence, I'm fairly sure this is not my car. Clarissa, do you ever have the sense—if this is crazy, tell me—that the world is haunted?"

Clarissa reluctantly agreed to move on, but after two more blocks in which there had not been another vehicle with Massachusetts plates, she wondered if they might not revisit the Honda Civic he had rejected.

"That's not my car," he said again, which was not exactly denying her request.

They retraced their steps in no particular hurry, their destination unacknowledged, and found themselves alongside the vehicle in question before either was ready to resume their postponed dispute.

She put her hands over his eyes, to which he made the smallest of complaints. "What does your lost car look like?" she asked.

It took him a while to evoke a picture in his mind. When he had conceded the car's loss, he had all but erased it from memory. "It's a grayish, tannish color," he said.

"What's the nameplate?" she asked.

"I don't pay much attention to those kind of things," he said. "It's a Honda something, a Honda Civic, I think, four years old, though it could be a Toyota. No, my previous car was a Toyota."

"When last seen, what kind of condition was the car in?"

"A few scrapes on the back and on the left side, which were not my fault," he said. "Other than that, and some winter residue, it looked almost immaculate."

"Well," she said, removing her hands from his eyes, "we have here a latish-model grayish-tan Honda Civic with a nasty scrape on the left side, and some scratches here and there on the back."

"All cars look pretty much alike these days," he said.

"Why don't you try your key," she said, "so there will be no residual doubt afterward."

He was in no rush to retrieve his key from the depths of his left pocket, but he made a point of walking around the car, going through the motions of noting its disfigurations. "This car has more dings than mine," he said.

She laughed. "I won't say it," she said, "because I don't want to have you angry with me again. If I didn't like you as much as I do, would I be here with you on this bizarre errand?"

He felt as if he were standing on his toes in quicksand. "What won't you say," he said, the words escaping his decision not to ask.

"I won't say what I won't say because you already know what it is. Look, I'm sorry, Josh. Really. I am sorry."

He produced the key from his pocket like a magic trick. With grave reluctance, he made a show of trying to open the passenger door and failing.

She gently took the key from him and opened the door on the driver's side on first try.

He turned away. "Must be a universal key," he muttered.

"I didn't hear that," she said, "but I get the general point. Shall we see if the key is also compatible with the ignition?"

She was one of those women who acted on the likely response to a question—he had intuited this about her from day one—before the answer was ever spoken. He put his arms around her, held her close to him—people passed in twos and threes, there were occasional cheers, darkness arrived unannounced—to hold off the inevitable for as long as possible.

"This," she said, "what you're doing, I had no idea it was coming. Really, no idea."

Years later, after they were living together, after they had done a scripted TV ad together for MatchesMadeInHeaven.com, in which he had acknowledged her as his soulmate, he still hadn't forgiven her for finding his car. That she knew he continued to resent her gave him a certain advantage in the relationship. For the first several years, before indifference set in, Clarissa did whatever she could to make it up to him for having occasioned his humiliation on their second date. With what she thought were the best intentions, the intentions of love, she had willfully done him a favor she might have known in advance he didn't want.

THE NIGHT WRITER

What can you say about someone who rewrites his sentences in his dreams? It has probably already been said. And it wasn't every night that he rewrote sentences in his sleep. Perhaps once a week or once every other week or once every three weeks—sometimes, in fact, two days in a row—whenever the subconscious compulsion took him, overriding discretion.

It usually happened on the road, when he was sleeping in strange beds, and came about more often than not when he hadn't had sex in a while, not even with himself. So what he did, was doing perhaps, was masturbate sentences. Was that what it was? Jerk them around to best advantage. Too often, when he woke after hours of sleep-ridden revision, exhausted from prolonged creative effort, only the worst versions of the sentences awoke with him. His memory, he had to remind himself, traveled poorly in the night.

During the day, his sentences resisted change, stared back at him defiantly, warned him not to fuck with them. And what would happen if he did? What could a sentence do to him that it hadn't already done? And why should it even concern him what his sentences might think? As they were his sentences, he could do with them as he liked. Couldn't he? Only if he had the courage to risk the unspoken dangers that lurked on the other side of turning them about. Not everything was susceptible to improvement, a former wife used to say. And perhaps nothing was, when looked at in a certain light. And the problem, as he saw it, as he badly defined it, wasn't something you could talk to your therapist or your wife about and expect useful response. And there was limited pleasure in it for him, revising sentences in his dreams, a few flashes of short-lived satisfaction, that's all. And when you weighed that transient satisfaction against the loss of much-needed sleep, the end result was less than nothing.

And then of course the product of his nighttime labors was always something less than itself in the morning, something or other slipping away. He kept a notebook and pen on an end table next to the bed to indemnify his altered sentences, but in the morning his writing implements were rarely where he had left them. One tended to fall to the floor on one side of the table, the other on the other side. They were like a bad marriage. By the time he retrieved them both, his sentence had miraculously restored itself to its original unsatisfactory form, and so there was nothing to write down. He imagined other remedies, kept a tape recorder at the side of his bed for a few days, but he had difficulty waking himself to speak into the microphone, which in no way violated his expectations.

So, refusing to give way to disappointment, he changed the nature of his goals. He would content himself with keeping his perfect (perhaps near-perfect) sentences solely in his dreams. It would no longer be a question of losing the sentence by not writing it down or recording it with voice. The sentence was there, living and breathing, unseen, unread, unheard, unwritten, in the ether of his dream. It was purer that way, more perfect (if perfect could be improved upon). And his alone, untainted by accommodation to the world outside himself, that world of potential readers that inevitably fell short of his expectations. And so those nights when, taken to heart by dreams, he revisited his oeuvre and reworked his sentences, he would be achieving a kind of nirvana unavailable to anyone else.

And one day, to which the above attests, he would write it all down, as he has, a lesser version of course of the improved sentences in his dreams, and whoever cared to look would be there to confirm the process and himself in the bargain, though probably not.

THE NEW YORK REVIEW
OF LOVE

Unequivocally adorable, aesthetically attuned, lifelong student of the arts, authentic, unpretentious widowed academic with an enchanting manner. Sometimes shy, sometimes daring, almost always delightfully unpredictable. A real head-turner. Fun-loving, though with the inner strength to keep afloat in good and bad times. Seeks attractive, fit, intelligent man with similar interests to share dinners, theater, opera, travel, the romance of life.

Dadora@headturner.com

Dear Unequivocally Adorable,

This is my first response to a personals ad and I confess to not knowing how to begin. I am, and I say this without irony, a bit in awe of your credentials. I have tended in the past to be wary of great beauties. In my youth, it was my practice to seek out the second-prettiest girl in the room, assuming she'd be easier to get along with than the reigning radiance. As you might imagine, this practice did not always yield what I was looking for. As I've gotten older, always a student of my experiences, I've developed greater respect for head-turning presences, realizing that outer attractiveness speaks, often eloquently, to the beauty within. You might say that I am a recent convert to the appreciation of someone who, like yourself, is "aesthetically attuned" and "unequivocally adorable."

I share some if not all of the interests you cite. I am a creative writer and intellectual who has recently retired from a successful career in advertising. I don't like to blow my own horn, but some of the wittiest and most compelling ads you've seen on television are my creations. Anyone who knows me knows that my true aspirations run deeper than the handiwork of my livelihood. Like you, I am a "lifelong student of the arts," theater and opera-goer, afficion of classical books on tape, reasonably fit, financially solvent, more than less charming with perhaps some of the same "inner strength" that has also kept you "afloat in good and bad times." Over the years, I've been happily married twice for extended periods of time, both marriages ending, unhappily, in divorce. *Casablanca* and *Realm of the Senses* are my two favorite films.

If I'm at all what you're looking for, I'd appreciate getting an e-mail from you at the above address. I'm looking forward to continuing our dialogue.

Sincerely,
Jack

Hi Jack,

I am pleased to report that I found your e-mail letter *mucho simpatico* and I've placed it high on the list of intriguing respondents. You were one of the few who didn't request a photo, but of course I'd be willing to send you one. We might, in fact, exchange images, if that's your pleasure. I am not someone who is attracted particularly to opposites, so I would be interested in knowing what plays you admire, what books you read for pleasure, the music that inspires you, your favorite museums, etc. If you had a weekend where you could do anything you want and do it wherever you wanted—a dream weekend, so to speak—what would be your choices? Also, please let me know how tall you are. Height is not in itself a requirement, so you might interpret this request as a symptom of curiosity and interest. Is Jack your real name or a *nom de plume*?

Cordially,
Deidre C

Dear Deidre C,

I was pleased to get your response to my response, and I can honestly say that you are also high on my list of prospects. As for my height, I am a shade under six feet, though I give the impression of being taller. If I had to choose a favorite playwright (twisted arm and all), I'd probably stick with Shakespeare, while giving a tip of the cap to Neil Simon. My tastes in music are quite various—classical, jazz, folk, rock and roll, opera, pop, almost anything by John Coltrane and Bob Dylan. And you? The dream-weekend question is harder to negotiate. I try to take every day as it comes, so as a rule I don't put off living life to the fullest for special occasions.

Okay—back to the wall, I'll give you an answer, which would probably be different tomorrow and different again the next day. My so-called dream weekend would take place on a well-equipped sailboat somewhere off the coast of Maine not far from, say, Islesboro, with an adorable and intellectual woman much like yourself and no other obligation than to take pleasure in the bay breezes and the incomparable sights and the sharing of affectionate companionship.

I'd be happy to exchange photos with you, but perhaps we ought to talk (through e-mail) a little longer before taking that next step. Is Deidre a real name?

Warm regards,
Jack

Hi Jack,

You must have been hanging out on my wavelength when you conjured your "dream weekend," and if I didn't believe you were an honorable person, I'd accuse you of reading my mind without a "by your leave." If you added "gyring in the waves" from this wonderful sailboat of yours, your proffered weekend would seem unbearably perfect. If I knew you better, and didn't have a care in the world, I'd have my bags packed in a trice and take the plunge.

Although I am a "can do" person, my life has not been a walk in the park. I've known my share of sorrow and I am on the whole a stronger person for it. I've mentioned in my published profile that I am a widow. In fact, and this is not information I give out to just anyone, I've been widowed twice. Again, let me say, I do not dwell on the unfortunate hands I've been dealt, but on my ability to triumph over adversity. As a child, I had an extremely minor case of polio, which has left me with a virtually imperceptible limp. My friends see it as a sexy adjunct to an otherwise adventurous and sensuous persona. Yes, Deidre is a real name but it is not exactly mine. My intimates call me Didi. What do your closest confidantes call you?

In friendship,
Didi

Dear Didi,

The voice in your letters, for whatever reason, seems uncannily familiar, as if I've known you without actually knowing you for as long as I can remember. For that reason, I want to strip away some of the artifice of the public self and give you a glimpse of the private person that lurks beneath. Sorry to say, I don't own a sailboat, not at the moment, but it has been a lifelong aspiration. No matter the word on the street, I am not without a few marginal deficiencies myself. I have never actually been to the opera, though if it's any consolation it is not an omission that I'm proud of. On the other hand, I am proud to say that I have persistently fought and virtually conquered my various addiction issues. I've not had a drink or whatever, social or otherwise, in eleven months and three days. Scout's honor. If, as has been said, I am a work in progress, isn't that what living is all about? As for my signage: I have been called Jack by my friends, but in the cause of total honesty I am compelled to say it is not actually the name on my birth certificate.

If the above revelations remove me from your radar screen, I'll make an effort, though not without a smattering of regret, to understand your position.

Best wishes,
Oliver

Dear Oliver,

I don't want you to think I'm as off-puttingly artsy and gorgeous as my original personals presentation may have signaled. My mother used to tell me ad nauseam, "Dorothy, always put your best foot forward." And I have, I believe, aspired to do just that. If one doesn't reinvent oneself every seven years or so, one can very easily disappear from the main stage. I was not, I confess, a natural beauty. Nor was I, as a teenager, the second-prettiest girl in the room, the one your younger self would have pursued. I was, I say without false modesty, somewhere in the middle of the pack. As I'm sure you know, intelligence and charm can more than compensate for nature's oversights. Also, I should say that I've always been attracted to men who are not in the least vain about their looks. I have generally held being "authentic" in the highest regard. So don't lose heart, Oliver. I await with pleasure the receipt of another of your lively, unassuming communications.

Your friend,
Dorothy

Dear Dorothy,

Is Didi short for Dorothy, or was Didi a different reinvented self altogether? And I do prefer being called Jack to Oliver, if you don't mind, the latter offered basically in the spirit of unmitigated honesty. That I tended to go after the second-prettiest girl in the room didn't mean I was always or often successful in that pursuit. I was not averse on occasion to settling for the second-homeliest girl in the room if she had a winning personality (as you seem to have) and was suitably affectionate. This is not to say that you are less than beautiful, though if you are it would not be a deal-breaker between us. Most men (and I don't exclude myself) like to have a beautiful woman on their arm not so much for the woman per se but for the macho statement it offers to the casual observer. With maturity, I've grown beyond that. What I'm looking for in a relationship is not just an adorable companion with whom to go to cultural events or the occasional Knicks game. I've come to believe that eros is also a vital component in any lasting relationship.

If we're not on the same page, I'd appreciate being so informed before we take our blossoming friendship to the next level.

Best wishes,
Jack

Dear Jack,

Whatever else I may be, I am not squeamish concerning sex. I've been known to call a fuck a fuck, the consequence be damned. If I'm no longer the intellectual sexpot of my younger days, when I was thought to be the Tuesday Weld of the academic set, I have learned a thing or two about love over the years. That you don't sail is not a problem; sailing, if the truth be known, has always made me seasick. Shall we meet, my friend? And if so, where?

Yrs,
D

Dear D,

How about the coming Friday at five at the Cedar Bar?

Yrs,
J

J, my friend,

I believe the Cedar Bar no longer exists. How about meeting in front of the former Cedar Bar, which is a short walk from my apartment. I have shoulder-length white hair and I'll be wearing a red sweater. And you?

Yrs,
D

My dear D,

I'll be wearing a black turtleneck and a gray tweed jacket. I have pepper and salt hair, what there is of it. To avoid confusion, I'll be carrying a black cane with an elegantly baroque handle. "This could be the beginning of a beautiful friendship."

Yrs,
J

APPETITE

First of all, don't believe what you've heard about me. Given the stories circulating, you would think I was some kind of retrograde chauvinist, but unless I'm suffering from amnesia or have been in a psychotic state for the past month, I know I've done nothing to warrant the current fuss. My lapses, such as they are, proceed from what might best be described as passionate excess.

When people refer to me as "larger than life," I don't think it's size alone they're referring to, though I am well over six feet and tend to weigh between 250 and 300 pounds depending on a nexus of variables. I have an oversized personality and an immense appetite, the one having only incidental connection with the other. This may sound like a rationalization, but I try to strike a balance between my needs—I am no stranger to restraint—and my underrated sense of decency.

Most women find me charming and that gets me in trouble. Four years ago, I was pressed to give up a tenured position at the University of Washington for having "inappropriate relations" with several of my women students. In fact, I never pursued a woman who hadn't made herself available to me first. The first of the women who complained about me to the authorities did so after I called an end to the affair. And though she lied about much of what happened between us, she never said I forced myself on her. One of the others—they came out of the woodwork like dust bunnies to testify against me—one of the more shameless others, said I had imposed myself on her against her will. It was her testimony and not the original complaint that turned me into a pariah. They gave me the opportunity to resign with the promise that my stigmatized behavior would not be broadcast elsewhere. I had no choice, my craven lawyer insisted, but to accept their terms. Anyway, even if I hadn't been pushed out, I was ready to leave Seattle, which was like living in the afterlife.

After the Seattle debacle, I took a slightly less prestigious job at one of the city colleges in New York.

There was this woman in my Life Drawing class, who tended to hang around my desk after the bell, chatting me up. An instinctive diplomat myself, I distrusted flattery in others, though this child-woman, Octavia, quite sexy in an unassuming way and probably the most gifted student in the group, had circumvented my alarm system. In fact, she reminded me of myself some years back, when I was starting out.

With Nora away for ten days, visiting her parents in Vancouver, I felt lonely and a tad deprived. Still (and I insist on this), I had absolutely no intention of getting involved with a student again.

On the other hand, I am an impulsive person, and one Friday when the saucy Octavia showed up at my office—ostensibly to discuss her progress in the course—I found myself inviting her to a weekend party at my country house, recently purchased and still in the process of renovation.

—That sounds fun, she said. Is there some kind of bus that goes there?

—You can ride up with me, I said. I'll come by and pick you up at nine on Saturday, if that's agreeable.

She accepted my offer with undisguised pleasure. It was only after she got into the car and discovered she was my only passenger that she asked who else would be there.

—Sam and Annie, I said, both of whom Octavia had met. They're driving up later in the day. Nora, unfortunately, is visiting her parents on the left coast and won't be able to join us.

I should mention that Nora and I, though not actually married, have been living together for twelve years.

Octavia rolled her eyes charmingly, withheld whatever rude remark passed like a shadow across her face.

—Anyway, small parties are the best, don't you think.

She glanced slyly at me as if taking my measure and I smiled back reassuringly.

She was mostly silent for the rest of the trip, and occasionally surly, preoccupied with whatever, so I told her some jokes, one of which provoked a laugh.

—You're impossible, she said.

—Yes, I said, and isn't that a good thing, which provoked further giddiness, all of which seemed a positive sign. In matters of the heart (or hard-on), I've always been a partisan of the implicit.

When we got to the house, we were the only ones there—actually Sam and Annie were not expected until much later (I was beginning to hope they wouldn't show up at all)—and noting Octavia's uneasiness, I made a point of being reassuring. I said that unlike some of my fellow shmearers in the art department, I was not the kind of man who sought affairs with his attractive female students. I let her know that the main bedroom was hers for the night and that I would put up in the airless guest room above the garage.

In the makeshift scenario of my imaginary movie, she would have said, Don't put yourself out on my account, but Octavia defeated expectation, thanking me in her sassy way for being a gentleman. I could understand that she didn't want to seem too available.

The house was a mess—we had left in a hurry the previous weekend—and Octavia seemed put out by the disorder. The first thing she did after checking out her room and changing into her bathing suit was wash the dirty dishes that had been left in the sink. I would have dried but I couldn't find a dishtowel, so I stomped about impatiently in the living room, cleaning off the couch, rearranging the clutter.

—You're very domestic, I said, but you're here to enjoy yourself. That's the point, isn't it? So let's have a swim and then we'll go to town for lunch.

—I can cook, she said, if you want to bring food in. Is there a dishtowel somewhere?

—Just leave them in the drainer, please, I said.

When I could finally get her away from the sink, we walked through a wooded area to the pond, which is at the far end of the property.

—How can I be sure you're not leading me down the garden path, said my witty flower.

—Is that what you think of me, I said, playing at being offended.

—I never know what's expected of me, she said. You'll have to tell me.

That was my cue (and didn't I know it), but I let the moment pass. I could tell from her expression that the pond, perhaps smaller and murkier than my description suggested, did not live up to expectations.

She sat down on her towel and opened a book she had brought with her while I launched myself with a rather graceful, I will say, surface dive. When I came up for air, I waved to her to join me.

—When I'm ready, she said, lying on her side on a skimpy towel in a provocative pose. I need to get some sun first.

There was of course no sun out, which I was discreet enough not to mention.

I did a few self-conscious, show-offy laps, imagined her watching my performance, then returned to her side.

—The water's perfect, I said.

—I'm getting hungry, she said, looking up from her book.

—Then let's go to town and get something to eat, I said.

—I want to finish the chapter first, she said.

I sat down on the grass next to her towel.

—If I were the author of that book, I said, I'd be terribly pleased at your devotion.

—If I were the pond, she said, I'd probably ask you not to be so rough with me.

—If you were the pond, I said, offering a mock sigh, letting the completion of the thought remain implicit.

At lunch she was again sullen and uncommunicative, and it crossed my mind that there was something a little off with the disconcertingly variable Octavia.

After I finished my burger, she was still picking at hers. Ultimately, she left more than half on her plate and it was all I could do not to ask for her leavings. The charmer anticipated me.

—Would you like the rest of mine? she asked.

—Thank you, no, the hungry man said, averting his eyes, but when she insisted a second and third time, I yielded to her seduction. Her burger was still warm from her touch when I picked it up.

2

We had just returned to the pond when Sam and Annie drove up in their black Chevy Blazer. Sam is a former MFA student and Annie, who I had a brief involvement with myself, was a life model in one of the classes he took with me. Usually the models don't mix with the students, but these two were living together with my blessing before the term was over. Octavia had met them both before and seemed pleased and even surprised by their arrival. Sam said they wanted to walk around town and invited Octavia to join them, an offer she accepted with more enthusiasm than seemed warranted.

So I had the house to myself for the next several hours, and I whited out a painting whose solution persisted in eluding me, then took a nap on one of the chaises on the deck. I must have been very tired, because I didn't hear them drive up.

—Do you know you have snakes on your property, Annie was saying to me when I opened my eyes. Her remark embarrassed me. I had a hard-on when I woke from some unremembered erotic dream and her snake comment I somehow thought referenced my condition.

Sam and Annie had brought back two six-packs of the aptly named Pete's Wicked Lager, which we took over to the pond with us. For the rest of the afternoon, we drank beer and lolled in the water. Octavia kept her distance in Sam and Annie's presence, which I read as a form of discretion. I asked her once as an aside if she were enjoying herself and she said, —I'm doing my best.

After dinner, which was barbecued trout and vegetable kebob, Sam and I went into town to get some more beer and we ended up at this pub that had a pool table and what with Sam bragging about how good he was, there was nothing to do but teach him a lesson. It took five games for me to assert my superiority.

When we got back—we had been missing for several hours—Octavia had retired for the night and Annie was on the couch in the living room, dozing over a magazine. She was angry with Sam when she woke and she insisted on going outside with him to discuss the matter.

—It's all my fault, I said.

In any event, Sam and Annie were planning to spend the night outside (under the stars, said Annie) in a sleeping bag they had brought for the occasion. My pajamas, which I rarely wore in warm weather anyway, were still in the bedroom and I considered retrieving them. I had second thoughts about disturbing Octavia, and besides, the eight beers I had put away had diluted my appetite for sex. So I moved my bulk to the room above the garage and fell immediately asleep in my underwear on a sheetless cot. I slept for about forty minutes, then found myself rolling from back to side, the small room, even with the one window propped open, without the courtesy of a breeze, and of course I had to pee. I had to pee with maniacal urgency. So I hurried down the stairs in my skivvies into the starless night and let loose my waterfall against the side of the garage. Assuming myself alone, I sighed with pleasure as I peed.

I wasn't aware of another creature coming up behind me until I turned around. It was very dark and I actually picked out her scent in the torpid air before I could make out who she was.

—Sam and I had a fight, she whispered.

—I'm so sorry, I said.

—It's all your fault, you know, she said.

—Yes, I said, I think I admitted to that.

—Oh, not tonight, she said, not the drinking particularly, though having a drunk boyfriend does not make me happy; but the whole thing, the getting together with him was your fault.

Although there was hardly more than six inches separating us, I could barely read her face in the dim light.

—That's the moment's disappointment talking, I said.

She laughed and I realized from the sound of the laugh that she had also been crying.

—You once said…, she said, and the next thing I knew she was up against me, her head against my cheek. You once said the moment was the only thing.

So we went up to my room-for-the-night above the garage to continue whatever had started of its own accord. The sex part was Annie's idea, though I will not deny I did not offer much resistance. She gave me head and, a gentleman in my fashion, I followed suit. To the best of my recollection, that's all we did. When I woke again at first light, I was alone in the room and could almost believe that I had dreamt the encounter with Annie.

I put on the baggy Bermuda shorts I had worn the day before and went down the stairs and into the house to brew a pot of coffee. Octavia and Annie were already there, squeezing oranges for juice and making pancakes on the electric griddle. There was no sign of Sam.

—You can take a shower now if you like, Octavia said.

What I really wanted was to brush my teeth and get out of the underwear I had slept in, which I did. I also washed my face and splashed some water on my private parts.

When I glanced out the window, I registered that Sam's Blazer was not where he had left it.

When I returned to the kitchen, Sam was stuffing his face with pancakes and the two women were gone.

—Did the women go into town? I asked him.

—Oh, he said, Annie and I had a fight. I would have won that last pool game if I hadn't been drunk.

—Of course you would, I said.

—So, what's going on with the two of you? he asked.

—Nothing, I said. What are you talking about, Sam?

—Come on, you know what I'm talking about, he said.

—You have my word that nothing much happened, I said.

—You don't have to be defensive with me, he said. I'm not Octavia's guardian.

So it was not Annie we were talking about. I sensed from the glance Sam gave me that he had also picked up on the implications of our misunderstanding.

It wasn't until about noon on Sunday that I found myself alone with Octavia again, Sam and Annie off somewhere in the Blazer. I was doing the crossword puzzle on the grass by the pond, distracted by her footsteps as she approached.

—How is it you're not off with Sam and Annie? I asked her.

—Are there any cunning country walks around here? she said.

—It depends on what you mean by cunning, I said, making a point of not looking up at her.

—Have I done something to offend you? she asked. If I have, I'm sorry.

Her question pricked a nerve.

—Why would you think you offended me?

—I don't know, she said after a moment's silence. I seem to have a way that I don't understand of getting people angry at me.

I looked up at her, trying to assess the ad hoc rules of the game she was playing.

—Give me a few more minutes with the puzzle, I said, and then we'll go for a walk if you like.

—I really think you're angry at me, she said, and made an event out of walking away.

I returned to the puzzle, but her presence or absence, my irritation with her performance, distracted me. After some procrastination, I got to my feet and walked back toward the house. I caught up with her on the wooded path, sitting on a tree stump, looking pleased with herself.

—Would you help me up? she said in a sulky voice, holding out her hand.

I should probably freeze-frame the action here to comment on what was going on with me. I assumed that the hand dangled in my direction was a sexual offer, belated perhaps but nevertheless whole-hearted and undeniable. I had of course been waiting with Jobean patience for this moment, so I was not about to turn her down. As I took her hand in my paw, my mind had already jumped two steps ahead and I was sorting out possible venues. At the same time, I was warning myself to stay in the moment—a sure indication that I had already lost it.

I can still see us, connected by our hands, Octavia moving to-ward me in mind-induced slow motion.

I remember bending toward her because of the disparity of our respective heights, feeling the strain in my back, tasting her mouth for the barest of seconds.

Her voice interrupted whatever was happening.

—I didn't ask you to do that, she said, did I? Did I?

—Of course you didn't, I said, and I lumbered away like some wounded bear.

She caught up with me at the end of the path and said she was sorry if I thought she had led me on because that had not been her intention. She even made a convincing effort at looking regretful, though I was not impressed. It was time for some truth.

—Of course it was your intention, Octavia, I said. It's what sepa-rates adults from children, taking responsibility for what they do.

—Wasn't my apology an indication of responsibility, she said. I thought it was.

—You might tell me what you had in mind when you asked me to take your hand, I said.

She smiled slyly, seemed about to explain herself, then teared up, mumbled something unintelligible, and sashayed off toward the house.

I was tempted to follow her, but instead I returned to the pond to cool off, swimming with a kind of demonic purpose, feeling at once immensely reasonable and unreasonably angry.

Sam and Annie were holding hands when they appeared at the pond about an hour later. They were going to take a quick swim and then make their way back to the city, taking scenic back roads.

—When are you planning to leave? Annie asked me.

—I tend to leave as late as possible, I said. It's an easier trip if you wait.

—Sam needs to get back, Annie said. Sam was uncharacteristically silent.

I had no inkling that the sky was falling when I trailed after them to the house to see them off.

On my return to the house, Octavia was sitting on a chaise on the deck, a book open on her lap. Her backpack, I noticed, was conspicuously positioned alongside the chaise. She seemed packed to leave, which was just as well.

—Your wife called about an hour ago, she announced, not looking at me. Nora, that's her name, isn't it, seemed surprised to hear a woman's voice and asked me who I was.

—Is that right? I said.

—I said, you know, that I was a student of yours, she said. I totally hope that was the right thing to say. I didn't want to get you in any kind of trouble.

—Not to worry, I said.

While Sam was packing the Blazer, Annie sidled up to inform me that in the spirit of being honest with each other, she'd told Sam about our late-night encounter.

I merely nodded, feeling a bit stupefied.

—Sam doesn't seem too put out by the news, I said.

—Don't be fooled by his manner, she whispered. He's actually furious. The reason we're leaving is because he feels compromised accepting your hospitality.

3

I was prepared for disaster when, the following Tuesday, the department head called me into her office for an unscheduled meeting.

The night before, I had what was probably the most literal dream I'd ever had or could remember having, in which, prophetically, I had also received an invitation to see the department head. In the dream, she showed me a handwritten letter including elegantly drawn illustrations ("elegantly drawn" were the head's words) from one of my students, complaining about my behavior.

—Before I bring you up on charges, she said, sticking her tongue out at me, I'd like to hear your response to the letter. She pushed the document across the desk to me, as if there were something so loathsome about it she could barely stand to touch it.

—Whatever's in the letter, I said, I want you to know that, given the situation, I behaved pretty well.

—Read the letter before you defend yourself, she said.

The handwriting was mostly illegible, and I wondered as I read the letter, or tried to read it, how much of it the department head had actually deciphered. What follows is what I remember of the document.

Dear Chairman Meow (the head's name was Dr. Kittman):

I am writing to you out of gentile (perhaps genuine) concern over {illegible} dis-something in our otherwise dis-something deportment (probably department). One of your {illegible} shmearers invited me to conjugate at his cunt-ry estate in the Catskills. There was supposed to be some kind of {illegible} and I believe, all things considered, I was inveigled (perhaps invited) to be the final course. I am not a tart no matter what {illegible} seems to think. He, the oppressor (professor perhaps), paints us all with the same tart brush. Frankly, I was shocked and offended to find myself in this man's crutches (surely clutches) when I had every right to expect that I had let myself in for no more than a peasant (no doubt pleasant) day in the woods. Ask anyone, my own {illegible} was totally beyond reproach. So what do you propose to do about this improprietous madder (surely matter).

Yours truly,
Anonymous Annie

—This doesn't make any sense, I said.

—Okay, she said. I just wanted to hear your side of it. You have my word, Tess Kittman said, that whatever is said here will go no further.

It was the heavy breathing quality of this statement that put me on my guard.

—You have the same assurance from me, I said.

—During the decision-making process right before we hired you, she said, we received an anonymous letter from Seattle advising us to turn you down because of certain imputed actions of yours at UW. As you see, we ignored the letter—you were otherwise such a strong candidate—though the charges against you did give some of us pause. When you hire someone, no matter how impressive the vitae, you never really know what you're getting. That's why we require a minimum of four years' service before we consider someone for tenure.

—A more than reasonable safeguard, I said.

—Well, yes, she said, though some more established people like yourself tend to find our policy somewhat frustrating. You're in your fourth year and I should imagine you'd like to know whether the department plans to recommend you for early tenure.

—I hadn't given it a thought, I said.

Throughout this mostly one-sided conversation, I had been waiting for Tess Kittman to produce Octavia's damning illegible (dream) letter. Instead she nattered on about rumors passing her way about inappropriate behavior on my part, but fortunately blah blah blah there had been no official complaints and the department (meaning herself), otherwise pleased with my performance, was nevertheless prepared to recommend me for "early tenure."

And that was it.

But that was not it. My radar accessed some of the floating rumors Tess Kittman alluded to alleging sexual improprieties, and I've had to deal with knowing smiles from a wide range of colleagues and students, some who had never even taken my classes. Octavia herself wore this sassy look on her face whenever our paths happened to cross.

As a consequence of unacknowledged anxiety, I've gained fifteen pounds in the two weeks following Octavia's country weekend.

Without telling anyone, not the department, not Nora, I've looked into other job possibilities, but there are no openings so far at the places I'd be willing to consider. If my financial situation were stronger, I'd take some time off from teaching and do nothing but make art. Sleep has not been a friend for the longest time. Whenever I go into the college to teach my classes, it is as if I am perpetually re-entering the landscape of my disgrace.

Look, if I don't know my own heart, who does?

If I were given to complaint, which I'm not, I would say cir-cumstances have conspired unfairly against me. I will not say it, but I think it, I can't help thinking it, and this deep sense of injustice, which comes unbidden, which whispers itself, provides a kind of pri-vate consolation.

Second of all, there is no second of all.

SUSPICIONS

The reason Julia didn't hire a private detective, apart from expense, was that she liked not really knowing what she was all but sure she already knew. Of course, there were also other reasons; principal among them was that she was not that kind of person. Or at least she didn't want anyone who knew her to suppose she was. But the main reason, the reason among reasons, was that she hadn't yet made up her mind as to what to do with what intuition told her were the hard facts she would one day have to face. And as long as it was merely a supposition, no matter how compelling a supposition, she was not obliged to do anything that would upset her becalmed marriage of twenty-two years. There was also the odd chance—the very odd chance—that she had misread the evidence littered in her path and that Henry, her psychology professor husband, was not using his ostensible Thursday night at the gym as cover for a relationship with another woman.

The above is what she told her closest confidant, Marcia A., needing to talk to someone other than herself, but that was before she had begun to suspect that Marcia was the one (or might well have been) her husband was seeing on the sly. The thing with suspicions is that, once you give way to them, they tend to occupy you like an infectious rash. "That's your guilt talking, honey," Marcia had said to her. "You can't put too much stock in anything your guilt tells you. You know that as well as I do."

"And what do I have to be guilty about?"

"What does anyone have to be guilty about," she said. "I only know what you told me."

WHAT JULIA TOLD MARCIA AFTER MARCIA SAID I HAVEN'T SEEN YOU
LOOK THIS HAPPY IN I DON'T KNOW HOW LONG

It's hard to talk about this because I don't understand it myself. I ran into someone at the AWP conference in Boulder, someone I once knew and hadn't seen in ages. Look, this is not to be repeated to anyone. To no one. Okay? You know, or maybe you don't, that I did a poetry writing MFA at Stanford in the seventies. I suppose everyone that goes into publishing saw herself in college as some kind of poet or story writer. Anyway, it was in my last quarter at Stanford that I got involved with one of my teachers. He was my instructor in a course in the metaphysical poets and was, not the least of his attractions, a poet himself. We got on very well, maybe too well, considering that he was married. I don't even remember how it started, but almost every afternoon we used to meet at my apartment and read poems to each other, mostly other people's, sometimes our own. We also made love, but I really think it was the reading of the poems back and forth that was our most indelible connection. I loved the way he read. He had unusual phrasing and he had this melodious voice. He was also very smart without being pretentious about it. I remember being impressed that he refused to call himself a poet even though he was publishing his work in prestigious places. He merely said that he wrote poems. I liked that about him. At the end of the spring quarter—this was something like thirty-one years ago, so my memory is vague on particulars—we separated while still being emotionally attached. I went to Paris, which had been an arranged thing long before we got together, and he took a job somewhere in the east, at Tufts I think it was, and that was it. We never saw each other again. That is, we never saw each other again until a week ago in Boulder, Colorado.

I never got to his reading, which I had checked off in the program listings as something I planned to attend—missed it accidentally on purpose, I suppose, by remembering the date wrong. I thought with a mix of regret and relief that I had avoided him, but he showed up at my event and came forward after my talk to present himself. He seemed greatly altered, not like an older self but like someone else altogether. I didn't recognize him when he came up to say hello, though I had the sense that I knew this man from somewhere. I was trying and failing to figure out from where so I missed much of what he was saying. He had affected a kind of scruffy style that I tend to find obnoxious, three days of beard, abbreviated ponytail—I think they call it a rattail—the bags under his eyes an advertisement for the romance of sleeplessness. And he was thicker, slightly stooped, with a modest paunch that said he had more important things to do with his time than keep fit—the phrase that came to mind was *pregnant with self-importance*—so that he looked every bit his age and then some. It was when he asked me, something in the voice, if I would have a cup of coffee with him that I realized who he was. Of course I already knew he was at the conference, but the image I had of him in my head was the long-lost, mostly forgotten version of him that in another lifetime I imagined I loved. It's possible that I had even seen a picture somewhere. On the back of his first book, possibly. I don't remember saying yes to his invitation, but as he had assumed my acceptance I saw no reason to disappoint. Thirty-one years had passed without a word between us. It was time to catch up, and surely there was a lot to catch up on.

So there we were, sitting across from each other in the Boulder cafeteria, making small talk with a kind of unearned ease that unsettled me. This time I was the married one and he wasn't, though he had three failed marriages to put on the table for my consideration. I was relieved at how painless it all seemed, and then he announced, forty-five minutes or so into our conversation, that he tended to think of me as "the great love of his life."

"No," I said, not because I didn't believe he meant it, but because I had once fantasized this very conversation and had, at some cost, willfully outgrown it.

And if his first confession wasn't offensive enough, he added, "For long periods I don't think of you at all, but when I do, it's always with regret at having lost you."

I got out of my seat in a hurry and stormed off. He caught up with me in the hallway outside of the cafeteria and apologized. I can't say why, but I put my arms around him then and we stood there— people walked around us to get by—holding onto each other. "No," I said again, this time in a whisper, though I continued holding on. "I hate your rattail," I told him, "and why the hell don't you shave like everyone else."

"Let's go sit in my car," he said, and I made an uncharacteristic noise that was meant as a laugh though failed its intention.

Instead of going to his car, which was a half-mile walk as it turned out, I went with him to his hotel room. It wasn't what you think. He was gentlemanly to a fault. We didn't touch in the hotel room but sat notably apart reminiscing—our memories often at odds—on what went on between us at Stanford. I made the mistake of confessing that I would have cancelled the Paris trip had he asked me to. "I thought of it," he said, "but I couldn't. I think you understand."

"I didn't understand any of it," I said. And I still don't.

I returned to my hotel room that night to sleep and didn't, re-playing our various conversations in my head, past and present. It was only after I resolved not to see him again that I fell asleep. Some-how we had breakfast together—I may have phoned him—and we spent almost all our uncommitted time in each other's company for the next two days, but that's as far as it went.

My flight was earlier and he waited with me at my gate and then gave me his card, which had his e-mail address. I gave him my e-mail on the back of a cocktail napkin. His parting words, which of course I remember, were: "Is it possible, Julia, that we're making the same mistake all over again?"

"Maybe it wasn't a mistake the first time," I said.

"Really I have nothing to feel guilty about. I almost wish I had. Nothing happened. I told you nothing happened. Why would I lie?"

"Obviously something happened," Marcia said. "Sex isn't the only currency between lovers. You know that."

"All right, nostalgia happened, but why should feelings of guilt come into play? I did nothing wrong. And I still don't think my sus-picions about Henry have anything to do with my brief encounter with this man."

"You can't even say his name, for God's sake. Is it a name I would recognize?"

"I don't think so, though it's possible. He's published a book of stories and three or four volumes of poems, though nothing in the last eight years."

"Do you appear in any of his work?"

"No…I don't really know. I've read very little of his work."

"You weren't curious?"

"Look, I don't know. I just didn't think about it."

"And why do I find that hard to believe? Do you want to know why I think you avoided reading him?"

He was coming to New York to see his daughter and he asked her if he could meet up with her while he was in town. She didn't see why not, or rather she did see why not but decided finally that it was better to see him than to avoid him. By denying him she had been holding onto him, or at least that's what Marcia seemed to think. So it followed that by not denying him, by spending time with him, she could get rid of whatever tenuous ties continued to bind them. Her goal, as she saw it, was to exorcise his ghost and perhaps at the same time, with any luck, keep him as a friend.

When she saw him waiting for her at Sixty-Fourth and Fifth, looking off in the opposite direction (she had been uncharacteristically late), she was thinking of how she would describe her first impression of him on approaching. The man waiting for me was not the one I was expecting to meet, she would say to Marcia. He was an imposter, someone who had stolen my former friend's identity. I had seen him as this older self in Boulder, but I nevertheless expected to see a considerably younger man waiting for me. Then he turned around. He turned around before I actually reached him and looked at me as if my being there surprised him. "What's wrong?" I asked.

"I didn't expect you," he said.

"I said I would meet you," I said. "Who were you waiting for if not me?"

"Should we walk along," he said, "or would you rather sit on a bench?"

Always decisions to be made. "I don't care," I said. "We can walk if that's what you want."

Though he seemed frail, he took long strides and I had to struggle to keep up. The wind swallowed whatever we tried to say to each other, which wasn't much. Anyway, it was hard to talk while walking as quickly as we were. At some point, a somewhat younger woman, coming the other way, called to him. I thought it must be his daughter but it turned out to be a former wife, which was not an altogether pleasant surprise. They talked a few minutes as if I were invisible and then she went on and we continued, though I found myself unreasonably angry at him.

"I'm through walking," I said.

"Do you want to sit down somewhere?" he asked.

"Not really," I said. "That line you gave me about being the great love of your life. I don't think so."

"I wasn't lying," he said. "If it offended you, I take it back."

His taking it back of course made things worse and I said some things that may have overstated what I actually felt. I gave him this tongue-lashing, called him a gigolo, accused him of issuing false compliments as a form of control, said he was the worst kind of woman abuser because he kept his hands to himself, and it kept getting worse until he said, "Please shut up."

Julia felt so bad she ended up apologizing to him, and they made up or at least went through the motions of reconciling before separating. She was sure that after her jealous rant he'd be more than happy never to see her again.

Nevertheless, he sent her an e-mail the day after he returned to Newton, which included the draft of a poem he was working on. At first she thought it was about her—why else would he send it?—which seemed consistent with his presumptuous stance in regard to her. On second reading, she saw that it was not about her at all, which in its own way was even more bothersome. And then she wasn't sure whether she liked the poem sufficiently to offer an opinion, not wanting to say anything she didn't feel. So rather than comment on the poem, she thanked him for showing it to her and sent back in exchange one of her own, one of her more recent efforts, something she had completed or stopped fussing with about five months ago.

The next day her poem made a return visit with a few suggested changes in italics under the original lines while making a meal out of how much the sender admired its sensibility. She accepted two of his five suggestions, made a few changes of her own (inspired by his critique), and, against her better judgment, e-mailed him the revised version. She had no idea what to expect, appropriate silence most likely, and was happily surprised to find a message from him the next time she checked. "Julia, it's terrific," he wrote, while making one further emendation, "and I hope you'll forgive me my unsolicited suggestions. It's what I do and it's a difficult habit to break."

Perhaps she was half kidding when she wrote back in apparent dudgeon, "If you're trying to seduce me with false flattery, you're barking up the wrong tree."

A day and a night passed before she got an answer to that one. "False flattery was genuine," it said. "And what gave you the idea I was trying to seduce you?"

"I'm glad you like the poem, along with the sensibility," she wrote back. "Your comments were helpful to me." She thought it best to let the seduction issue die of its own accord.

A twice-weekly e-mail correspondence followed, a period in which Henry's presumed transgressions seemed increasingly provocative.

One Thursday, an hour after Henry had left for the gym, she called Marcia, who had gradually emerged as Julia's prime suspect. Marcia answered, seemed uneasy, said she couldn't talk at the moment and would call back later, which provided Julia with the evidence she had told herself she wasn't looking for.

To avoid obsessing about Henry and Marcia, and not wanting to concede any more of her life to the time-killing distraction of TV, she decided to phone the man she had e-mailed a new poem to that very morning.

He picked up on the fourth ring and seemed, this professed devotee, not to recognize her voice. She had identified herself as "me," assuming (and why wouldn't she?), given the intimacy of their dialogues, that "It's me" was sufficient calling card.

He was discreet enough not to ask who "me" might be, hoping, she assumed, he would figure it out along the way. Betrayed on all sides, she resolved to give him no help. Several minutes into the conversation she said, "You don't know who this is, do you?" But saying that in just the way she said it—she listened to its echo—was a tipoff in itself.

"I'd know you anywhere," he said

"Right," she said, laughing without amusement. "You still haven't called me by my name."

"I thought the point was, we didn't use names," he said. "You never call me by my name."

It was true that she didn't. "That's because you're an imposter," she said. The silence on the other end troubled her. "I didn't mean that the way it came out," she said, as close to an apology as she could get without humiliating herself.

"I am an imposter," he said, "but you weren't supposed to know that."

"It takes one to know one," she said.

"Look, I haven't read your poem yet," he said. "I was just about to pick it up, really I was, when you called to check up on me."

"I called because I wanted to hear your voice," she said. "I don't mind that you haven't gotten to my poem, but if you love my work, as you say, I'd think you'd want to read it as soon as it arrived."

"I wanted to clear my head before looking at it. You might say I've been saving it in the way a child saves a favorite food for last."

"What a sweet thing to say," she said. "Would you tell me if in fact you didn't like my poem?"

"Since I tend to like what you do a great deal, there's virtually no chance of that. I will tell you if I think your poem needs work. Does that satisfy your question?"

"It might," she said. "We'll see."

"Why are you so distrusting?"

"Is that what I am? I might ask in return, why all the extravagant compliments?"

"I'm not aware of what you're referring to. You seem to think that I'm insincere, which is certainly unflattering to me."

"I'm sorry," she said, regretting the apology, which seemed to have made its way on automatic pilot. "I think the problem is that, whatever else is going on between us, we don't know each other well enough to have the conversations we've been having."

"Of course we do," he said. "Otherwise we wouldn't be having them, would we? Where's your husband?"

"He'll be back in about thirty minutes. This is his extracurricular night out."

"His what? What are you telling me?"

"It's just an idle suspicion. Henry is a good man."

"I believe he is," he said. "You wouldn't have married him if he wasn't. You wouldn't have stayed with him this long if he wasn't a good man."

"Come on," she said. "I'm not as perfect as you pretend to think I am. I've been known on occasion to make mistakes. Particularly, you might say, where men are concerned, I've been wrong once or twice."

"Sometimes good men also cheat on their wives."

She heard herself laugh while not being especially amused. "Are you talking about yourself now?"

"I'll take the fifth on that one," he said. "It's hard, I know from personal experience, to carry around unprovable suspicions concerning people you're close to. I'm sorry."

"My friend, Marcia, thinks it's all your fault."

"My fault? How so?"

"You should know," she said. "I thought you understood me better than that. Marcia thinks it's because I feel guilty about meeting you that I've taken it into my head that Henry is having a fling."

"And what do you think?"

"In my worst moments, I believe it's Marcia that he's seeing. At other times, at the same time sometimes, I think I'm probably wrong about that."

"What do you believe at this moment?"

"Do you really want to know?"

"I wouldn't have asked if I didn't want to know."

"At this moment, I believe he's in bed with Marcia even as we speak. I'd like to drop the subject now.... Actually, I hear his key in the door, so I'll get off. Bye."

He hung up without a word, or perhaps she had cut him off. She had called to suggest that they meet again, perhaps in the Boston area this time around, but it had never gotten said. And besides, she would have to get an assignment from the magazine to make such a trip possible without having to lie to Henry or, which would be even more difficult, having to tell him the truth.

Marcia called her at work to ask if they could meet for lunch. "The reason I didn't get back to you last night was that a friend was over. Someone I had met in an elevator of all places."

"Was it anyone I know?" Julia asked.

"I don't think so. He's some kind of lawyer. Actually, he's quite nice for a lawyer. I'll tell you about him when I see you."

Julia listened for subtext, but heard only what she was primed to suspect and perhaps not even that. The earliest they could get together was the following Monday.

The magazine was sending her to the Athenaeum in Hartford to interview the new director and she e-mailed her old friend, mentioning the assignment, offering it as an opportunity to get together. Since their extended phone conversation, she had not received an e-mail in almost two weeks.

Late in the day, when she had all but given up hearing from him, she got her answer. "As much as I'd like to," he wrote, "I'm going to say no. I've spent hours shaping my reasons for you, but I suspect sending them to you would probably be redundant. I believe you understand probably better than I do why I can't (or won't) show up in Hartford to see you."

"You give me more credit than I deserve," she wrote back. "It would not be redundant to tell me why you won't come. There's a lot I don't understand, your reasons not the least of them."

A week passed without response, and she went off to the Athenaeum wanting to believe that he would show up unannounced and explain his silence, or apologize, or both. Or something. His almost presence haunted her day and a half in Hartford, and she found herself missing him and furious at him and expecting to run into him at every turn.

On her return, she wrote a draft of a poem about being rejected at a museum while standing in front of a portrait of George Washington.

At lunch with Marcia, whom she had either forgiven or no longer suspected of treachery, she said there seemed a kind of raw justice in his breaking off with her this way since it was she, walking on imaginary glass in Paris, who broke off their correspondence thirty-one years ago.

"And what about your suspicions concerning Henry?" Marcia asked.

"What suspicions?" she said. In any event, they seemed less troubling now. Whatever Henry was into, he was not going to throw her over on the basis of nothing much or whatever and perhaps she had imagined Henry's sly infidelity because some part of her wanted him to behave badly.

Marcia, on the other hand, was more interested in her own story at the moment.

And then, how many months later, I noticed his name in someone else's copy of *The Village Voice* while riding the subway home from work. I wondered if it was a misperception, so I picked up a *Voice* from a freebie distribution box when I got off the train to check it out. When I thought of him, which was not often, which was not all the time, I worried that his extended silence betokened failing health. Why else would he stop writing?

It took a while to find the item, but Julia had seen what she had seen. He was in fact giving a reading of his poems—he was the featured reader in a group of three—in a small theater in the East Village from a new book recently published. And why hadn't he mentioned that he had a book coming out? It was possible that he had and she had been too self-involved to take it in. She was eager to hear him read but she was uncomfortable with the idea of him seeing her in the audience, which invited—she was no stranger to the experience—a kind of decisional paralysis. A late-hour choice: she called Marcia and urged her to go to the reading with her.

"Oh," Marcia said, "I wish I could. I have something else on that I have to go to. I so much wanted to see what he looked like."

And so the burden was all hers. And, after two other unsuccessful calls, after going back and forth on the question, she decided to go to the reading solo.

She arrived late—a male reader in his early fifties was at the podium—and she stood in the back until the performance was concluded. At first she didn't look for him and then when she did, when she methodically searched the crowd, she didn't see him anywhere.

There were six rows of folding chairs, eight to a row with an aisle in the middle. It was a substantial crowd for a downtown poetry reading. All but three seats were taken—two of the unoccupied chairs in the first row, which had always seemed to Julia like putting oneself on display. Nevertheless, in the brief interstice between the first reading and the second, she ducked into one of the empty seats in the first row. The second reader was a younger woman who had recently published her first book. She read with her eyes on the page in a hushed, somewhat embarrassed voice. There was a shout of "louder" from behind Julia and the reader looked up from her text as if she had been slapped.

The procedure, it seemed, was for each of the poets to introduce the succeeding one. Though there was still no sign of him, the second reader, with considerably more aplomb than she delivered her own work, introduced him.

A flash of guilt passed through Julia, as if in imagining the worst (and how different, really, were imaginings from wishes?) she was responsible for whatever version of it had come to pass.

He walked on a cane, though made an effort to appear vigorous, taking exaggerated strides as he approached the podium, entering from some back room where he had no doubt been gathering his strength.

Though he had what she thought of as "hospital pallor," he looked younger somehow than the last picture of him she had filed away in her memory. He caught her eye and smiled at her or at the woman on her left or at the elderly couple directly behind her.

This is the fantasy she had while she half listened to him read his passionately ironic verse with a worked-up energy that seemed hollow and perhaps even desperate, his musical voice cracking from time to time: She imagined herself taking a sabbatical from work (also from her marriage, which was harder to conceive) and moving to Newton to look after him. If he was dying, which seemed at the very least a possibility, she would stay with him until the end. Otherwise—this second scenario was more difficult to envision—she would care for him until he was on his feet again, however long it took, and then return home or stay with him, whichever seemed at the time the right thing to do. In any event, she sincerely doubted Henry would take her back after her leaving him as she had no matter what she decided.

The last poem he read was about a man waking up in a hospital room after an operation and perceiving himself in some version of the afterlife commensurate with what he deserved. The last part went something like, "The ghost he was rose from his bed and crawled hand upon hand into the greater dark."

When the reading was over, he got an extended ovation that moved her to the verge of tears. She had to wait in line to get to see him—he was stationed behind a table, signing books, a younger woman she had seen in the audience posted alongside him. She had no idea what their relationship might be. In resisting jealousy, she found its impingement inescapable.

"Julia," he said to her when she handed over his book for him to sign, "I can't say how grateful I am that you came." She exchanged suspicious nods with the younger woman standing to his right. He

seemed even more deathly pallid up close. "Oh," he said after returning the signed book, "this is my daughter, Kate. Kate, this is Julia,
who was a student of mine at Stanford over thirty years ago." A nod
was exchanged between them.

"Kate," she said, taking a step to the side in prelude to walking
away, feeling obliged to say something, "your father was absolutely
the best teacher I ever had."

Though she usually resisted such extravagances, she took a cab
home without once glancing at the inscription he had written. Henry
was waiting up for her, watching a movie on television when she arrived.

"I was at a poetry reading," she told him, "by a poet who had
once been a teacher of mine."

"I wondered where you had been."

Julia removed the book she had been carrying in her purse and
handed it to her husband, who was a talented reader of poems, for
his inspection.

WALKING THE WALK

Every morning, he gets up earlier than he had the day before, eager to get going with nothing in particular to do. He is exploding with energy, is still a young man despite chronological evidence to the contrary. The house echoes with silence and it is a priority to him to escape even if it means walking in the dark, even if it means the defeat of inevitable return. If there were somewhere else to go (there must be, he tells himself, though his memory is not what it was), he would not come back. He is the only one out there, walking in the half-light (the half-dark?) who doesn't have a dog with him as an excuse for his escape. The regulars say good morning or nod to him when he passes or look through him, wondering what he is doing out so early without the obligation of a dog at the end of his leash.

He has thought of getting a pet, has imagined himself walking a dog, but that's as far as it's gone. If he knows himself at all, he knows he wants the dog only for the duration of the walk itself. After returning home, he and the dog would likely have nothing to say to each other. The dog would have to be fed. The dog would bark. The dog would wander around his house looking for something to occupy idle paws. A perfect solution would be to borrow a dog from some as yet nonexistent service on a daily basis to accompany him each morning, a dog that might be returned without much difficulty when their otherwise companionable walk was concluded.

While walking unattached, solo as it were, his own dog, he sometimes wonders in his daydreamy way—his mind full of useful detours—if it wouldn't be an interesting career move to create the very service he has been deprived of. "Walker Dogs: companions for the lonely. With the loan of a Walker Dog, you'll never have to walk alone again. Canine companions in all weight classes."

That's not the story he has set himself to write. In the germinal concept that inspired him to set words to page, Tristan, his protagonist, would meet someone, something would happen, a relationship formed—perhaps only in the imagination, which is the best kind for someone who has trouble getting along with others.

Impeded by an almost imperceptible limp, a limp his most recent former wife used to make note of, Tris is committed to walking as briskly as he can for thirty minutes every morning regardless of weather, the worse the better. The slap of wind keeps him on his mettle.

"You're out early today," she says to him after the "good mornings" have been exchanged.

"You too," he says, but since they are moving in opposite directions, circumstance forecloses further conversation.

She takes turns running and walking her medium-sized, nondescript pet, occasionally singing to him or to herself. The dog's name is something like Winnipeg. Something about the youngish gray-haired woman, whom he thinks of also as Winnipeg—names of people are rarely exchanged on these walks—engenders fantasy. He knows most of the dogs' names on his walk and none of the owners' names. He wonders if they, if she, thinks of him as the non-dog man.

In his fantasy scenarios, Winnie is a single owner, but one morning he discovers Winnie's dog attached by leash to someone other than the woman he has reinvented as an obsession. This is the first time he has seen the dog with someone else, a disconcerting revelation. It is not a husband walking the dog but another woman, a notably younger woman. They pass each other without acknowledgement, though the dog makes an abortive move in his direction.

When in the course of his perambulations their paths cross a second time, Tris says, "Good morning," and is answered in kind. "I've seen that dog with someone else," he says.

"That's possible," the woman says, moving on, and in the aftermath of this inconclusive meeting, he wonders if he's misidentified the dog.

"Is her name Winni?" he calls after her.

"She's a he," she says, stopping briefly to answer, no further information offered.

He modifies his scenario. Winni's owner, the eponymous Winnie, is sick or busy and her younger sister, visiting from Ohio after a trial separation from her husband, has agreed to walk the dog in her place.

When he gets home, he gives the scenario another twist. Winnie, that is Winni's owner, is older than she looks, and the young woman walking the dog in her place is actually her daughter. This daughter, name to be discovered, has come home to stay with her mother after her marriage has come to an unlikely and surprising end, her husband leaving her for another man.

Winifred (called Winnie) tells her daughter, Angela, that bonding with a dog (her own experience with Winnipeg confirming testimony) has a way of healing one's sadness. And so as an initial step in the recuperative process, she lets the unhappy daughter take her sweet-tempered dog for his morning walk.

"How did it go?" Winnie asks when Angela returns.

"It was like almost fun," Angela says. "I met the non-dog man you mentioned and he gave me the distinct impression that he missed you."

"Why would he miss me?" Winnie asks. "I mean, we hardly know each other outside of a few random encounters."

"I think he has a thing for you, Mom," she says. "I really do. He gave the impression of being really disappointed that you weren't there."

"You think?"

Nevertheless, the next morning, when the non-dog man—he has begun to think of himself as such—crosses Winni's path, the dog is attached to the daughter, Angela, once again.

This time after they exchange "good mornings," Angela stops briefly to let him pet the dog. After the vagaries of the weather have been sufficiently noted, she mentions that the woman he usually sees with the dog, the dog's owner in fact, is her mother and that her mother sends her regards.

Such news would have surprised him had he not already imagined the possibility of an intuitive sympathy between himself and Winifred. "Well, then when you see her," he says, "thank her for me and give her my regards in return."

"Absolutely," the daughter says.

While waiting for the mother to reappear, the non-dog man discovers he is also attracted to the daughter, something that might well be a problem later on in whatever relationship develops with the mother. That Angela stopped to talk to him suggests, or so he wants to believe, some kind of rudimentary interest in him despite the obvious difference in their ages.

He tells the daughter, a coded confession, that of all the dogs he meets on his morning walk, Winni is far and away his favorite.

The next day, or is it the one after that, he is almost surprised, though not unpleasantly, to discover Winnie once again connected by stretch leash to his favorite dog. She seems pleased to see him—all those back-and-forth regards exchanged have changed the aura of their relationship—and, though usually careful not to give himself away, he responds in kind.

"I've missed taking Winni for his constitutional," she tells him, "but Angela needed him more than I did. He's been a great help to her."

"That's a great dog," he says, for which she thanks him with some embarrassment, which he finds charming.

Instead of taking his usual route, he elects to turn around and accompany the two Winnies in the opposing direction. They exchange generalized personal information as they walk along together, the dog between them like a chaperone. Winnie is a songwriter, she confides, who has had some professional success. After she sold her first song, she rashly quit her job as a copywriter, assuming—incorrectly, as it turned out—that she was moving into a new and lucrative career. Seven months later, she was again writing advertising copy, though working longer hours at a slightly reduced salary.

He is more interested in hearing her story than relating his own, though common courtesy demands he give something of himself back. "I also write," he says. "That is to say, I used to write."

"Are you a journalist?"

"No."

"Well, what is it that you write? Is it some kind of secret?"

"In a way," he says. "My books are a kind of secret, though that's never been my intention."

"Books? You said books, plural, right? How many are there? I'm impressed with anyone who gets published. Do you write mysteries? I'll tell you right off I never read mysteries, so I probably wouldn't have heard of you."

"I write fiction but not mysteries," he says. "And there's no reason you would have heard of me. How many songs have you written?"

"A lot," she said. "Do you really want a number? I've written something like twenty-seven. Four of them have been picked up, a fifth is being considered."

"I'll tell you what," he says. "I'll give you one of my books in exchange for one of your songs."

She doesn't answer right away and it strikes him that his offer has embarrassed her. They watch her dog squat to relieve himself with the kind of attention usually reserved for museum walls or auto accidents. While she deftly collects the turds in a blue plastic wrapper, he looks off into the distance.

Their conversation continues on his computer screen after he returns home, somewhat disappointed by their first extended encounter.

"How long have you been living alone?" she asks him.

The odd thing is he can't remember how long it is, so he gives out the first number that comes to mind, which is eight months. It is actually closer to two years.

A somewhat awkward dinner invitation follows, which he accepts with guarded eagerness, though, as he remembers later, he has something on for the same night so he has to call to change the date. He can tell from her response that she doesn't trust his excuse. "I'm hoping for a rain check," he says.

"I'm not sure I know what that means," she says, "but okay, if that's what you want." Nevertheless, no replacement dinner invitation is made.

When he doesn't run into her the next morning, he can only assume that she has changed her route in order to avoid him.

He checks his watch and discovers that he is ten to fifteen minutes later than usual, which may explain missing her or may not. He replays the pivotal phone conversation in his mind and it never comes out the same way twice.

Women have had a history of misunderstanding him. Which may also mean that he has a history of sending out messages to women that are susceptible to misreading. Or, without being fully conscious of his motives, some part of him wants to send the wrong messages.

A somewhat familiar voice interrupts his self-concern. He sees the dog first, brushing up against his leg, before he recognizes Angela at the other end of the leash. "How are you this morning?" she asks.

That's one of those questions he never has the answer to, so he pets the dog as a time-consuming diversion. "Where's your mother?" he asks to fill the silence.

"I'm afraid there's only me today," she says. "Is that a disappointment to you?"

"Why would I be disappointed?"

"Actually, my mother's not feeling so well."

"Sorry to hear that," he says. "Tell her I hope she feels better."

"Ah-ah," Angela says. "She will feel better if you agree to come to dinner tomorrow night."

When someone invites him somewhere out of the blue, he usually says he has to check his calendar to see what else he has on, but this time he says, "What time do you want me to come?" He is not going to make the same mistake twice, or if he is, he is not going to let himself know it.

He arrives five minutes early carrying a bottle of red wine that is somewhat more expensive (perhaps even better) than the ones he usually delivers to dinner parties. Angela lets him in, offering him a hug he is not fully prepared for.

Twenty minutes go by—they sit in the cramped living room, drinking white wine and looking for a subject on which they might have something of interest to say—without an appearance by their hostess. Presumably, Winifred is in the kitchen preparing dinner. Still it seems to him odd that she hasn't at the very least stuck her head in the room to say hi or whatever.

Between them, they finish the bowl of mixed nuts—mostly stale peanuts, as it turns out—which represents, as he sees it, the hors d'oeuvres course. He hopes he hasn't killed his appetite, but the meal has been a long time in coming.

He resists inquiring on Winnie's absence, though he gives muddled consideration to the question, self-consciously aware of the awkwardness of his situation.

He evokes, insofar as memory allows, the wording of Angela's invitation. He thinks dinner was mentioned, though under oath he wouldn't swear to it.

At last, Tris says in the voice of uncontrolled desperation, "Is your mother going to hang out in the kitchen all night?"

His question seems to surprise Angela. "My mother? Didn't I tell you, Tris? Winnie's not here. Winnie had a job-related appointment for tonight she couldn't get out of. She sends her regrets."

He doesn't know what to say and so says nothing while wondering what the hell is going on. By this time, they are on their second or is it third bottle of white wine and he is not sure whether muted outrage is the appropriate response. Should he be flattered that Angela wanted to have him over despite her mother's absence? "Is there anything to eat?" he asks.

"Oh," she says. "The reason I didn't serve anything is that I'm on this diet. Should I get you something? I didn't realize you were hungry."

"It's all right," he says, not wanting to be trouble or wanting to be more trouble than he knows what to do with. "What's available?"

They go into the kitchen together—that is, he trails after her—and Angela swings the refrigerator door open for his inspection. "Tada!" she says.

Perhaps not. There are lots of bowls covered in plastic elbowing each other among the crowd of jars and plastic containers. His own refrigerator has virtually nothing in it. This is the antithesis.

"You can have anything you want," Angela says, "but I have to say that a lot of it is probably past its prime. My mom can't bear to throw anything away. It has an odd smell, doesn't it?"

The decision seems to make itself. "You know, I think I'll go," he says. "Thank you for…" He has difficulty completing the sentence. "For putting up with me."

"It was really nothing," she says.

When he gets home after picking up a slice at Mamma Roma's, a poor substitute for the homemade dinner he had allowed himself to anticipate, he imagines that Angela, not wanting to be left alone, says, "There's no need to run off," and takes his hand and leads him into the smaller bedroom—her mother's guest room—where she has been staying during her visit. He thinks to say to her that this, whatever it is, is inappropriate and not what he wants, but, on the other hand, not having had sex with another person for a while now, it is what he wants—it is exactly what he wants, there is nothing he wants more—and so rather than lie to her, he shyly accepts her tacit offer.

After extended foreplay, they are just getting into it when he hears the outside door open, and someone, Winifred no doubt, enters the house. He freezes, regrets everything.

"Angela," a voice calls.

"I'm here, Mom," Angela says. "I'm in my room." Footsteps approach.

He revises his scenario. After a peck on the cheek at the door—actually, an extended kiss initiated by Angela, the kind of kiss it would be poor manners not to respond to—he manages to get out of the house unscathed. Before leaving, he gives Angela his card—the last one of a pack he had made up twelve years earlier, the one he had been holding onto for just such an occasion—which includes his various contact information.

When Winifred opens the door, he has this determinedly innocent look on his face and has one shoeless foot on the floor. Winifred makes an incomprehensible noise—something between a sigh and a scream—and covers her face with her hands.

Angela says, "Please, Mother, I'm a big girl now."

He leaves Angela without another word spoken between them. Winnie is sitting on the couch, her eyes averted, as he makes his endless journey to the front door. "I thought you would be home," he says.

Winifred says nothing until he has his coat on and is making his escape, has one foot out the door.

"Why don't you take Winni with you," she says, "and keep him for the night. I'll make up a plastic bag of dog food for you and I can give you a sheet of instructions. I'd like you to have him for the night. I've been thinking about this for a long time."

Though her offer puzzles him, he doesn't ask for an explanation but takes the proffered leash and the bag of food. It is the least he can do after his unseemly transgression.

At first, he is touched by her kindness. He now has a dog to legitimize his thirty-minute morning walks. Still, when he gets home, despite the meticulous instruction sheet Winifred has typed out for him, he worries he has gotten himself into something he is not equipped to handle.

He decides to take Winni on a tour of the house to acclimate the dog to his new surroundings. The six-room excursion takes seven minutes and a handful of slow-moving seconds to complete, leaving a large chunk of time still unsubscribed. The dog seems mostly bored in his company while being a good sport about it, and Tris considers returning him, though he doesn't want to admit defeat.

He usually reads before going to bed for the night, but with the dog on hand he decides to watch some TV instead, an activity that might possibly also include his guest. Include may not be exactly what he means. Distract, perhaps. He doesn't really believe that a dog, no matter how intelligent, has enough attention span to sit through an entire movie. Nevertheless, feeling desperate, Tris runs through his commercial-free movie channels, hoping to hit on something that might catch Winni's attention while beguiling Tris at the same time.

What he needs, he decides, is a film in which a likeable dog plays a prominent part. Something like *Turner and Hooch*, which he has seen random moments of over the years while browsing channels, looking for something else. At first go-around, there is nothing appropriate outside of one of the *Thin Man* sequels on TMC, which he stays with for a while, directing Winni's attention to Asta whenever the famous terrier scampers mischievously across the screen. Lying at his feet, the dog glances at the movie only long enough to dismiss whatever it is Tris is staring at, more taken with watching him watch than with the images on the screen.

When Tris, after nodding off at the very moment the murderer is revealed, goes upstairs to bed, the dog trots after him as if they had known each other forever. As he undresses to get into his pajamas, prelude to flossing and brushing, the dog watches him with a quizzical look on his face. Shortly after he falls asleep, maybe two hours later, the dog barks, startling him awake.

He has difficulty falling asleep with the dog, a stranger really, sitting stiffly just a few feet away, giving off vibes of displacement. "It's all right, Winni," he says, and the dog gets up from his squat and licks Tris's hand, which has been hanging over the side of the bed. At once touched and revolted, Tris turns on his side facing away and gives up nagging consciousness for a few moments of oblivion.

When he wakes at whatever time, he discovers with a pang of pleasure the dog lying, paw over his eyes, on the rug alongside his bed, moaning softly in his sleep. "It's okay, Winni," he says as he steps over the dog, careful not to wake him, to get to the bathroom down the hall. On his return, the dog is missing.

"I didn't realize," Winifred says, back-stepping out of the room and shutting the door behind her.

"What a mess!" Angela says as he sits with his back to her, slipping on his pants. "I don't know why it is, but I've always had a thing for mother's boyfriends."

"We had too much wine," Tris says.

Dressed, he holds out his hand for Angela to shake, but her focus is inward. "Anyway, nothing really happened," she says.

Before leaving, in a rueful state, he repeats his wine excess explanation to Winifred, who seems almost willing to forgive him. "My daughter is in a vulnerable state," she says sternly, her arm on his shoulder as she escorts him to the door. "I hope you'll be kind to her."

"I missed you," he says. "It was you I came to see."

"Go on," she says, pushing him out the door.

He discovers Winnipeg sitting by his bowl in the kitchen, after a bout of concern that the dog had gotten out somehow and run away—or worse, that the dog had in fact never actually been there.

Though he is apparently waiting to be fed, Winnipeg walks away from his food after Tris fills his bowl. "Come back," Tris calls after him, but then notes, on the instruction sheet, "that sometimes Winnipeg will not eat in a strange house and not to worry about it." Nevertheless it takes a while for him to shake off his disappointment and even, to some extent, hurt at having his meal rejected.

When Tris goes into the living room to collect the dog's leash as prelude to their conjoined morning walk—the main event, as he sees it, of their limited time together—he hears crunching sounds coming from the kitchen. Winni is apparently eating his food. So: not a strange house after all, he tells himself with perhaps inordinate satisfaction, restraining the impulse to wave his fist before an unseen audience.

As he is fastening the leash, as instructed, to the ring protruding from the dog's collar, the phone rings. He considers not answering, can say afterward that he has already gone out, but the insistence of the ringing gets the better of his resolve.

As expected, it is Winifred on the line, setting up a place and time for them to meet and exchange the dog. "Was it a good visit?" she asks.

When he finally leaves the house with his borrowed dog for his morning walk, he feels a sense of well-being unknown to him for as long as unreliable memory extends. He is by nature too cautious, too aware that every high has a low waiting in the shadows to take it down, to name the feeling happiness.

Nevertheless, it is undeniably pleasure to him to share a connection with this other creature while traversing on a warm pre-spring day the handsome streets of his Brooklyn neighborhood. His only regret is having agreed to the exchange with Winifred, which awaits him—checking his watch—twenty-three minutes down the road.

Only for a few minutes does he wonder what the others think when they see the non-dog man with a dog, with a dog they recognize as belonging to someone else. He can imagine the scenarios a passing owner-and-dog, who have seen him many times in his usual dogless state, might take away from the encounter. The obvious conclusion is that he is in some way connected to the dog's owner, a friend no doubt, probably a romantic involvement, possibly a live-in boyfriend, which is, the passerby would surmise, a late-in-the-day development.

The first dog to cross his (their) path is the Shih Tzu, Lulu, with her oversized owner, and they seem unimpressed with the change in his status, the owner muttering his usual "good morning" while keeping his dog from contact with Winni. The next dog, a spaniel mix, merely crosses the street when they see him coming.

Not sure of the protocol, Tris keeps Winnie close when larger, meaner-looking dogs approach. On occasion, barks are exchanged.

He oversees Winni's urination with an encouraging compliment, pleased at their mutual accomplishment.

And then, as he dreamed he might, he manages to pick up Winnie's poop in a blue plastic bag, imitating the deftness of others he has observed.

The business part of the walk out of the way, Tris goes off in a new direction, matching his increased pace to Winni's. After a while, he enters what he thinks of as unknown territory.

At some point he realizes, glancing at his watch, that he is nearing the time for the exchange while being a considerable, unspecifiable distance away from the appointed spot.

He wants to keep going, doesn't want to give up the dog, but it is hard to reverse a history of doing, more often than not grudgingly, the expected thing. So he turns around and to the best of his ability—sense of direction not one of his natural skills—attempts to retrace his route. Several blocks pass as they hurry along, guided by urgency. He doesn't so much look at his watch as his watch, on its own recognizance, glances at him, making him aware that the appointed time for his meeting with Winifred has passed. On two different occasions, he thinks he sees her in the distance, shortening the space between them.

He is surprised that Winifred accompanies him out the door, her hand still at his back. "Let's take a little walk," she says. "Okay?"

He nods, without words, locked in regret not so much at what he had done as being caught almost in the act of doing it.

She takes his hand as they walk the same streets he has walked by himself every morning. "I know you didn't mean what you did," she says. "At least I hope I know that."

"Thank you," he says. "I also hope I didn't mean it."

She lets go of his hand. "And what is that supposed to mean?"

"I'm trying to be honest with you," he says. "I don't know why I went into the room with Angela." He reaches for her hand, but she hides it behind her back.

"I'm not sure that honesty is what I want from you at the moment," she says. "And I don't want to hear any more apologies."

Her saying that silences him. The only words that offer themselves are in the nature of regret. If they keep walking together, he suspects, inspiration will extend his vocabulary.

"I'm not forgiving you," she says.

"No?"

"Not at all."

"Then why are we taking this walk?"

She pushes him away from her and he staggers with comic exaggeration as if her fairly gentle shove had considerably more force.

"You had that coming," she says, "and I think you know it."

"I had worse coming," he says, finding her hand and pulling it to his side. He waits in suspended time for a teenage couple to move past them.

"I'm warning you," she says, "if you try to kiss me, you're looking for trouble."

He lets her threat hang about on the periphery of consciousness before digesting it. Time passes. She makes a point of taking back her hand and returning it to the sanctuary behind her back. They turn the corner. This street is darker than the one they abandoned. After a few more idle steps, sensing his moment, he risks everything.